THE ILLIAD CHRONICLES

The Lich of Izaman

Clinton Reel

Cover designed by Milau

Clinton Reel
Website: https://clintonreel.com/
Twitter: https://twitter.com/clintonreel
Facebook: https://facebook.com/thereelclinton
Mailing List: https://clintonreel.com/mailinglist

Printed in the United States of America

First Printing: Aug 2018

ISBN: 9781983164415

The world is often filled with darkness.
Sometimes, someone will enter your life to light the way.

CONTENTS

CHAPTER I

It was one of the darkest, stormiest nights in a hundred years, at least that is what the doomsayers were saying. If it were any darker, one could mistake for the Darkening occurring once again—for the second time in a month, an abnormal occurrence. The trees within the forest of Kala were being whipped around at high speeds, causing many trees to topple over and crash to the earth below.

It seemed as if the rain would never stop.

Within moments of the strong storm beginning, lakes were forming within the water basins, quickly causing them to overflow into the nearby residential areas. Some of the nearby villages foresaw what was to come and evacuated before it began. Many, however, decided to ride out the storm; their homes now completely flooded, with an untold number seemingly to have perished by the flood.

Perched atop a nearby hill, Jacqueline was sitting against a solid, dry rock she stumbled upon. She knew she was fortunate to find a place to stay, but she wished he could help the denizens of the people below. However, the young assassin knew she had to keep her mind off that; she had her wounds to attend to first.

Her wounds cut deep into her skin across her left arm, with some bleeding profusely. Scratches and bruises were also scattered around her body, a reminder of her bloody showdown. Jacqueline winced in pain as she attempted to wrap a cotton bandage around it.

"Damned goblins," she cursed, talking to herself. "If only I were more careful."

Days before the storm arrived, Jacqueline had heard stories about how goblins were pillaging, raping, and murdering villagers to the eastern side of Zalzabar. With each village she visited, her disgust only grew and grew as she saw, first hand, their mark on her lands.

Each of the villages told the same story of hate, malice, contempt, evil, and darkness. The villages were razed to the ground in a burning inferno, with many of their citizens trapped within the very buildings they once thought as safe. Burned, charred remains of human corpses littered the village streets, with many being desecrated by the very beings that slaughtered them.

On each of the bodies were three small symbols etched into their foreheads. While no known mortal could comprehend the language of the goblins, Jacqueline had seen enough to know that it was the mark of one group: The Scavengers. They were known far and wide for their hatred towards the mortal races of Ethos, going as far as to killing themselves only to kill others.

Jacqueline hunted down the Scavengers for days—possibly even a week—in search of their home. She scoured the country-side, searching high and low for the hideout to those who did evil to the Zalzabarans.

Her efforts were eventually rewarded when she was able to find their base of operations in the mountains. Littering part of a plateau was a large army of goblins with half-made tents, half-eaten remains of animals, and kegs of drinks. As her eye trained towards the center, she could also make out larger, more well-made tents—most likely belonging to the leaders of the Scavengers.

Before the assassin began her assault, Jacqueline scouted out the area for several hours, searching for key weaknesses in their defenses. From guard postings to routes of incoming and outgoing Scavengers, she waited patiently to find the critical flaw. All she needed was one, and she found it in the explosive exla barrels surrounding their camp.

When the next day dawned, Jacqueline jumped into action. As the goblins continued their day-to-day operations of mining the mountain, eating whatever meat was available or even sleeping, Jacqueline worked to prepare her strike. However, to her misfortune, a massive storm was brewing to the west—she had little time to spare.

As the sun was setting, and the Scavengers began to retire for the evening, Jacqueline fired several large fire-enchanted arrows towards the barrels. Upon impact, the barrels exploded, and a chain reaction started.

The mountains shook like a giant earthquake as each barrel detonated like dynamite, causing every goblin in the area to awaken and run around screaming, looking for answers. Rocks and massive boulders fell from above, crushing several goblins unlucky enough to be beneath them. Goblins unlucky enough to sit next to the barrels were disintegrated into ash.

She fired two explosive-enchanted arrows to the center of the camp, sending around twenty goblins flying in each direction. Jacqueline could remember the rush of adrenaline consuming her body as she jumped towards the goblins from the mountaintops. As she drew her twin daggers, Jacqueline sliced and cut each of the goblins within seconds. With each death, another two followed as the assassin quickly jumped and sprinted towards each of her enemies.

Several of the goblins quickly reacted and rushed their attacker. Most of the slashes and jabs were quickly countered, resulting in another goblin falling over as one of Jacqueline's twin blades pierced their chest. Several of the goblins were able to sneak attack the assassin with bludgeoning weapons, causing her wounds to appear. In anger, she lashed out in a powerful fury that eliminated the rest of the Scavengers within moments.

Within only ten minutes, the entire Scavenger camp was destroyed. Their legacy was all but a memory, now. Jacqueline prayed to the unanswering Gods that the souls of those affected could rest easier.

Jacqueline shook her head. She couldn't tell how long she daydreamed. Seeing the seemingly permanent darkness surrounding her caused the young adventurer to question her mortality once more. Just like most mortals on Ethos, they were tired of the constant threat of evil, hatred, and even war. Ever since the Gods disappeared over a thousand years ago, it seems like that's all Ethos knew.

That's all Jacqueline ever knew.

Then, her mind wandered to the sins she committed. She often grimaced in the fact that she once symphonized for the Chaos Order. When she joined their ranks, she thought their cause was righteous and just—one that was meant to unite the many races of Ethos. However, as time went on, she saw the atrocities they caused to even their own kin. Not only were the niyans and the Children of Sin seen as weaker, inferior beings, but so was anyone else who didn't commit to the Order.

While the world—no, the entire realm—were always appalled by the acts of evil the Order committed against the niyans and the Children, Jacqueline also saw what they could do to everyone else. In a lot of ways, the Order was not too different from the Scavengers Jacqueline had just slaughtered.

With the ever-rising threat of the Nightmares, Jacqueline felt the only way toward them off forever is to unite Ethos. However, with the Order continuing their age-old war against the other alliances, that dream seemed just like that: a dream.

The young assassin sighed as her head hit against the sturdy rock. Jacqueline knew she was only one piece in the grand scheme of things, and—while she was skilled—there wasn't much she could do against her former faction. There is a reason they had survived for over a millennium.

But, deep down, she knew she committed evil. In a lot of ways, she, too, wasn't much different from the Scavengers.

Jacqueline only hoped that, maybe one day, the amount of good she did would outweigh the amount of evil she had caused.

Unfortunately, she knew that might never happen.

———

Jacqueline jolted awake as the world around her shook with the boom of a mighty thunder. Since she arrived in the cave, the storm had not quieted down. In fact, it seemed like it only got worse and worse. There was no telling how long she had been there, or how long the storm had left.

"Lightoa."

A small, warm light appeared above her and illuminated the cave once more. For many people, it was dangerous to use a spell without a scroll, but, fortunately, Lightoa used very little Energy. Even as someone not accustomed to the ways of spellcraft, it was easy for one to cast a small light to illuminate the dark. Still, only a small portion of the cave could be seen.

A sizeable stream of rainwater had seeped in from the ongoing storm and flowed deeper into the dark depths of the cave. Stalagmites and stalactites were randomly scattered within the cave itself, their shadows cast against the cave walls. As she looked into the shadows, she swore she saw a shadow move. She stared in the direction of the shadows for some time before deciding otherwise.

Jacqueline went over to the steady stream of water and kneeled next to it. She splashed her face several times and rinsed her short dark blonde hair out. As she rinsed it out, she could see a small amount of red falling from her scalp. Investigating further showed it was merely dry blood, most likely from her encounter from the day before.

As she was rinsing off the dirt and debris from her right arm, Jacqueline looked up and saw several drawings she hadn't noticed before. She got up and walked over to the drawings, confused on how she had not seen them before.

The drawings seemed to be done with a sort of white substance, possibly chalk. They had a small glow to them, causing them to be seen even in absolute darkness. To the left, it depicted five men riding atop their horses. Each of them wielded a different weapon: a sword, an axe, a mace, a bow, and a javelin. Above their heads were also the symbols of fire, water, earth, wind, and light in the ancient language of Atrian.

The five horsemen were charging to the right where a single, large drawing was. It was mostly faded, but Jacqueline was able to make out that it looked to be a skeleton with a large staff. Surrounding the skeleton were much smaller undead creatures, mostly skeletons and wisps. Above the head of the skeleton was the Atrian symbol of darkness.

The cave suddenly lit up in a blinding flash, followed by a large, crashing boom that echoed across the sky. When her vision returned, Jacqueline could no longer see the drawing. It was gone! But, how?

Jacqueline looked around. Was she going crazy? Was it the lack of sleep? She could feel her eyes growing heavy, so maybe it was hallucinations?

She shook her head and walked back over to where she was resting before. Using a large rock as a pillow, Jacqueline rested down and stared up at the ceiling, still puzzled by what had just happened.

Soon enough, her eyes closed.

Just as she could feel her body start to drift off into sleep, she felt another shiver go down her spine. The air around her grew cold, and she was starting to shiver. The temperature change felt unnatural—as if being controlled by another.

Slowly, Jacqueline opened her eyes. She looked around the cave, but there was nothing there. The adventurer summoned another small light to brighten the area. When she did so, Jacqueline screamed for a moment and jumped backwards to the wall.

"What do you want, ghoul!?" she ordered.

Outside of the range of her light spell was a floating, nearly transparent skull. Around the skull was a light red aura, one of which Jacqueline had never seen before. In some ways, it seemed like an illusion, but she could feel a powerful magical presence radiating from the ghostly apparition.

"The return… Comes…" the ghostly creature answered.

"What?" she questioned. "Return?"

"Soon… The stars of this world… Shall disappear… For the time… Of shadows draws close…"

The ghost disappeared. She peered outside of the cave and could see that the storm had stopped. She went to the front of the cave and looked outside. The Great Moons—all six of them—reflected off the large lakes that had formed from the storm. Were it not for the destruction it had caused; it would be a beautiful sight.

However, all she could think about was the ghost and their   words.

CHAPTER II

Jacqueline hardly slept the rest of the night; dawn came far too early. When Sacrilege, the mighty sun of Ethos, peaked over the western horizon, the humidity slowly started to climb. By the time Jacqueline had woken up, she could already feel sweat overtaking her body.

"Wonderful," she said, groggily.

The young woman stretched for a moment, then grabbed all her belongings—it was time for her to move. One of the elders in the nearby towns had to be told of her success, so they could finally rest easy.

In her mind, Jacqueline was already determining how the conversation would go. Most of the villages in the area were poor and lived in worse poverty than she had ever gone through, but she felt they would still attempt to offer her an award. Most likely, it would be through Rubees, but it wasn't outside the realm of possibility that they would offer someone as a servant to her. Or, even worse, a mate.

Zalzabarian villages, due to their small capital, often bartered and traded goods and services. If they couldn't, they would offer something else, usually their own bodies. Jacqueline—even though she grew up in Zalzabar—didn't necessarily agree with this system, always wanting one to follow their own free will. Even if it was seen as disrespectful to decline a gift from an elder, accepting a life was the last thing she would do.

Still, she had to practice each scenario in her head, over and over. The large hill she found herself on gave her plenty of time to rehearse the scenarios in her head.

By the time she reached the bottom of the hill, her clothes and armor were drenched in sweat. The humidity, however, only continued to climb. The large pond at the base of the hill, at least, was becoming shallower.

Zalzabar, being the most north country in the massive continent of Ayasha, often saw brutal winters, but it also received as brutal summers on occasion. Lately, all it has been is warm, causing many of the inhabitants of the country to retreat into their homes until the evening. Many people from the outlying villages have passed out, and even died, due to the intense climate.

In fact, the biggest festival of the year—the Ak'aha—was put on hold in fears of more people passing out or dying. It was the first time in multiple millennia since the festival was postponed. When Jacqueline learned of the news, it dampened her spirits as it was one of the many ways she and the Zalzabarians could join for peace, food, and drink. It gave them an opportunity to keep their minds off the countless battles and wars being fought.

It didn't affect her for long, however. Not too long after the Ak'aha was postponed, the assassin heard of the Scavengers in the east and quickly moved in. Jacqueline had little time for emotions, which is why she always preferred to work alone.

Moving in the shallow parts of the water proved difficult for her, often causing Jacqueline to second guess herself or where she was stepping. The water was murky and dark brown color, making it impossible for her to see where she was going. One wrong move and she could easily get stuck. Or, she might fall. What made it worse was that Jacqueline hardly knew how to swim.

Eventually, she was able to make her way up another hill. As she did so, Jacqueline reached for her pocket and pulled out a whistle. The whistle was unremarkable, being made of iron and oak with a small emblem of a horse on the side of it. She blew into it, giving off two long, loud notes with a moment's pause between.

Not too long after the second note, a large white horse flew through the hillside. If one had an untrained eye, they would only see a white blur coming for them. As the blur grew closer, it started to slow down until it eventually stopped. Jacqueline's horse—Ramadier—had beckoned to her call.

Ramadier was of the mesia breed, some of the fastest horses in all the realm. Obtaining one was a difficult task, but the benefits for an adventurer such as Jacqueline was too good. To compliment their speed, the mesia were also intelligent creatures, often showcasing this as the horse saved Jacqueline's life.

"Hey, boy," she greeted, reaching up to pet the horse's muzzle. "Ready to go?"

In response, the horse turned to the side for his master to climb up. Jacqueline jumped high into the air and landed on the leather saddle. She grabbed the reins of the mesia and began to look around.

If she was correct, the nearest village was to the south. Once the adventurer located the sun, she turned Ramadier towards the south and snapped his reins. Jacqueline quickly braced herself as Ramadier's speed picked up. Within moments, he was at top speed—they would arrive in no time.

————

Around an hour had passed, and the two finally arrived in the village of Wao. They were greeted with a small sign showing the name of the village, with two additional signs pointing to Zamia and Armia in separate directions.

As the two strolled into the village, there were several groups of kids playing games. One group was kicking a rubber ball around, another was racing one another around the village, and a third was playing a simplified version of race-ball, a complicated game combining aspects of kickball and racing. As Jacqueline looked around, some of the zichan and human children looked back at them with curiosity.

As one would expect, there were no thorans or niyans here. The thorans were once the Order's slaves, being used for all sorts of acts from mining, cannon fodder, or even as experiments in their search for the "ultimate lifeform." Luckily, the thorans were liberated several hundred years ago, and have since joined the North Star and Dragonean Alliances in their quest to defeat the Order. Still, it wasn't abnormal to find thorans living in Order-aligned lands.

The niyans, on the other hand, were the sworn enemy of the Order. The Order has existed for most of recorded history, but it wasn't until the Gods' disappearance that they turned to the mass genocide of the niyans. The niyans, to the Order, was filth and must be destroyed.

She didn't know what she was expecting, either. If a niyan was found on Order soil, not only would they be executed, but so would those harboring them. There weren't many places in Ethos where the races could live together in harmony.

The village itself was unremarkable, with many of the homes being made from broken bricks, rotten wood, or

17

tattered tents. In the center of the village was a larger tent that was in a slightly nicer shape—albeit that wasn't saying much. On the sign in front was one word: "Elder."

Jacqueline hoped off Ramadier and made her way towards the entrance of the tent. Even after all this time, she hardly knew how she would respond to their rewards.

Before she could speak, Jacqueline heard the low hum of a woman from within the tent.

"Enter."

Hesitantly, Jacqueline obeyed. As she entered the tent, a wall of stench hit her. The smell was almost overwhelming, smelling of a musty body odor and candles, and caused Jacqueline to wave her hand to try and alleviate the stench.

Sitting in a chair in the center was an elderly woman, whose eyes were closed. They wore a long grey tattered robe that extended towards the ground. There were small gold bands on their wrists, with a similarly gold band around their neck. On their forehead was the emblem of an eye. This woman was a Seer!

As soon as she saw the emblem, Jacqueline bowed as a sign of respect. There weren't many Seers left on Ethos, but those who survived were revered as saviors to their people. There was little doubt that this old woman knew why Jacqueline was here.

"Thank you, Jacqueline," she began. "For what you have done for us... For us all. The spirits of those long since passed, at last, rest easy."

"It was my pleasure, mighty Seer," Jacqueline said.

"Unfortunately, we have not a reward to give."

"A reward was never my intention, ma'am."

The Seer smiled and opened her eyes. She stood up and approached the young adventurer with a fondness. It was obvious that she appreciated the words, as many would have demanded one, even if they had nothing to give.

The Seer's smile, soon, turned to a frown as she turned around. She coughed several times into a handkerchief, then turned back towards Jacqueline, still frowning.

"I'm sorry, dear," she apologized. "But, I am afraid we have need of you once more."

Jacqueline shook her head.

"Anything, mighty Seer. My swords are at your command."

The Seer nodded her head several times and walked over to a chest at the corner of the room. They opened the chest and rummaged through it for some time. Eventually, they pulled out a small tome from the chest and closed it. They opened the book and began to look through its contents. At last, the Seer turned towards Jacqueline once more with the book open.

"Have you... Ever heard of the Lich of Izaman?" she asked.

Jacqueline hesitated for a moment, thinking back to the stories she had read over the years. However, the Lich of Izaman did not ring a bell. Jacqueline shook her head in response.

"Meredith Graha was her birth name, but she soon turned dark," the Seer began. "Once upon a time, in the Fifth Era, a vast shadow eclipsed the land of Hian. That shadows soon extended to the west, then eventually to the north. Within three years, Meredith, the Lich of Izaman, had cursed the land. The skies were blood-red, the water was a pale purple, and the moons ceased to be. The creatures of everlasting darkness—the Nightmares—beckoned to her command, and her command alone."

The Seer coughed a few times and turned over to the next page. Jacqueline's eyes widened as she saw the depiction of the Lich in front of her. The night before, a ghastly creature had appeared in front of her. That ghast and the Lich were one in the same!

Tha-that's impossible.

"But, a hero rose from the north," continued the Seer. "A hero of pure heart, a hero of pure courage, a hero of pure light. They challenged the Lich of Izaman. And, after a brutal showdown, defeated Meredith."

The Seer closed the book and handed it over to Jacqueline. Jacqueline took the tome in her hands and looked down at the book's title: *The Dawning of Evil.*

"When the Lich was slain, all that was left was her mask. It could not be destroyed by normal spells. As well, the mask often turned its controller mad. Powerful men and women would hear the voices of those long since dead, eventually turning their heart dark.

"The mask was too powerful and was locked away in the Tomb of the Lich. Three magical barriers were placed on the tomb in the hope that the Lich's power would never be seen again."

There was a silence in the room. Jacqueline, still staring at the book, looked up at the Seer. Before she could ask her question, she already knew the answer.

"Someone had disturbed the tomb?" she asked.

The Seer shook her head.

"Worse… Her resurrection has already begun."

CHAPTER III

It had been several days since Jacqueline left the village, with most of the journey to the capital city of Zala having been spent reading a tome. The cover of the tome was heavily weathered, with corners missing. On the inside, there were several strange symbols she had never seen before. Ever since she acquired it from the Seer, she had spent most of her nights trying to decipher what they said.

The Seer—to Jacqueline's confusion and dismay—did not know what she was speaking of, as if she couldn't see the archaic language in front of them. Were the symbols just illusions, just like the skull she saw before?

Tomb and *Lich* were often repeated in the text. It was obvious this was all referring to the Lich of Izaman's final resting grounds, but it would not tell her where, exactly, it was. The text she could read was just mentioning her story and her fall from grace.

Jacqueline placed down the book; she had to have read it a dozen times in the past week, if not more. She rubbed her eyes and looked around in the large stone library. Zala was said to have one of the best libraries in the massive super-continent of Ayasha, but even they had little information on where the Lich could be.

In fact, there was little information about the Lich in general. Whatever she could find only mentioned the Lich in passing, not going in-depth on what they did. Jacqueline partly wondered if this was a coincidence, or if this was something else entirely.

She could feel her frustrations rising. Jacqueline was entrusted to defeat or destroy this great evil, but she hardly knew where to start. All she had to go off was the tomb, which wasn't entirely helpful.

Then, it hit her.

What if I am looking in the right place? What if they are hidden away?

Jacqueline got up from her seat and walked down the endless aisles. For several moments, she continued to walk around the library, the flickering of the torches being her only source of light. Every so often, there was a burnt-out torch, causing her to have to eventually summon a light to illuminate the path ahead.

After what seemed like hours, she came across a different section of the library. The aisle was dusty and filled with cobwebs. Most of the library was warm and humid, but this part she stumbled upon was cold and dry. Jacqueline couldn't explain it, but there was a sudden change in the air as she came up on the aisle—as if something magical awaited.

Slowly, the young assassin approached. With her last light having flickered out, she quickly summoned another to assist her. On each side of the aisle, there were dozens to hundreds of ancient books, most of which rotted, weathered, or burned.

Some of the books also had a chain and lock placed around them—possibly meaning they held forbidden knowledge, too dangerous for the world. The books that weren't locked, when picked up, began to deteriorate in her hands. She was forced to take better care of the books she picked up. After a while, all she could do was pull the book out slightly and hope it had a title. Almost every book held no title, or the text was too faded to read.

All except for one.

The last book on the row looked newer. It was black with red highlighting certain parts of the cover design. The chain was made of a different type of steel and was new—all the other chains could be removed with minimal force. Behind the chain was the image of a skull, one that looked very similar to the one the assassin had encountered before.

Jacqueline peered around, seeing if there was anyone near. When the coast was clear, Jacqueline reached into her small bag and pulled out a key. The key was attached to a small red, spiked chain that she wound around her wrist.

After doing so, she pulled on both ends as hard as she could, drawing blood and invoking a wince out of her.

Skeleton keys were some of the most sought-after devices in a thief's arsenal, being able to unlock any lock they desired—most of them anyways. However, to use such a device, one had to use their own blood to activate it. Otherwise the key wouldn't work. Part of the existing Energy was also sapped, weakening the user.

However, it was all worth it if the book would lead Jacqueline to the Tomb of the Lich.

The adventurer placed the key into the keyhole slowly. After a few moment's pause, the key began to light up. She turned the key slightly until she heard a click.

Success.

The lock opened, allowing Jacqueline to remove the chain. Quietly, she placed the lock on the nearby mahogany shelf, doing her best to ensure the metal didn't clank against itself and draw attention to her.

Once again, she looked around to ensure the coast was clear. Then, she started to open the book to its first page. In the middle of the page, there were four words: *Tomb of the Lich.*

Jackpot.

Jacqueline slowly squatted to the floor, then sat down, flipping through the many pages. The book was heavier than she had realized, causing her to almost fall when she was going down.

She quickly glanced through the pages, reading small parts of each sentence as fast as possible. With possibly little time until she was found, Jacqueline had to study as much as she could on the Lich.

Most of the pages she read were about the various stories involving the Lich of Izaman. From their origin story, their first kill, their first resurrection, and even their last battle. Every detail on who they were, who they could've been, who they became, and the extent of their powers was written down.

On the last handful of pages, Jacqueline found what she was looking for. There was a large, mostly dated map of Zalzabar towards the back. Towards the center of the country, there was a small red x. While the map wasn't entirely detailed, Jacqueline knew that the x was in the Ila Mountains.

"Well, well, well," whispered a voice from the darkness. "What do we have here?"

Jacqueline quickly glanced up. She had expected to see the librarian standing there, but instead saw a mysterious hooded figure barely visible through the veil of shadows. In their left hand was a lantern, only barely making out their silhouette in the darkness. In their right was a blade with a green liquid at the end of it—poison!

Jacqueline threw the book to the ground and unsheathed her two daggers. She put the daggers in front of her face, crouching slightly as she got into a defensive stance. That was the only response she would give.

"It's… Unfortunate I have to do this to you, Jack," said the voice. "But, my Lady demands it."

"Jack?" asked Jacqueline, slightly startled. Her startled look quickly turned to anger as she bore her teeth slightly. "How do you know my name?"

The hooded figure threw their lantern into the air. When it landed on the ground, the glass shattered, and the light disappeared. While Jacqueline couldn't see, she could hear something running towards her at a high speed.

Trusting her instincts, and her reflexes, Jacqueline stood her ground. She could hear a blade slicing through the air, aiming for her abdomen. With one of the blades, she parried the attack, and, with the other, struck at her foe.

Her opponent withdrew for a moment, cursing at Jacqueline. Their voice started to turn gravely, with a low growl coming from their lips. Hissing passed through their lips as they stood back up.

Jacqueline took the opportunity and cast a third light spell above her, this time using slightly more Energy to extend its duration. When it illuminated the area, Jacqueline could see a small pool of blood going away from her.

The hooded figure pulled back on their cloak, revealing their facial features to the young adventurer. His eyes were slanted slightly with two fangs extending from their upper jaw. On their forehead—to Jacqueline's surprise—was the symbol of a bear.

"Zane!?" yelled out Jacqueline in surprise.

Questions started to flood her mind, causing Jacqueline to lose her concentration. Why was Zane attacking her? How did he get to Zalzabar? Why was he here? Was he working for the Lich?

"Fucking bitch!" yelled out the niyan. "I'll kill you!"

Jacqueline snapped herself out of her spell and stayed her ground, still in her defensive stance. While she normally never lost concentration in battle or allowed herself to be fazed by another's words, having Zane—her childhood friend—attack her was a sort of psychological struggle she never dealt with before.

The niyan rushed back at Jacqueline then started to take several more slashes and jabs at her. By the time Zane reached Jacqueline, she had mostly snapped herself out of her spell. Every time the niyan swung, it was parried, blocked, or dodged. She could've countered and ended the fight easily, but she had questions he needed to answer. All she could do was continue to evade his attacks and hope his stamina diminishes enough for the assassin to subdue him.

Her opponent kept their assault for several more moments before Jacqueline noticed their swings and jabs getting slower. Jacqueline switched to offense and jabbed one of her daggers into their arm connecting and piercing through their flesh instantly.

The niyan screamed out in pain, shrieking as the blade exited their body. He dropped his poisoned blade and fell to the ground. Eventually, they curled up into a ball and sobbed as Jacqueline overlooked them in sadness and confusion.

"Just what happened to you, Zane?" she asked. She shook her head several times, trying to think of reasons as to why the normally timid niyan would act out in this way.

Then the air changed. A certain electricity, a certain power, filled up the air, causing Jacqueline's shorter hair to stand up on end. The air continued to intensify, and the temperature began to rise. Before long, it felt like a sauna from the heat.

The niyan roared loudly—one that rivalled an Abomination's with relative ease. Their eyes began to change colors from their natural green to red, shifting between the two colors for some time until it stopped on red. His muscles began to expand, and fur began appear suddenly.

Jacqueline jumped back. She was hoping they wasted their Energy fighting her, but it looked like she miscalculated Zane's stamina immensely.

Niyans were a unique species in that they could transform into their "spirit animal," at the cost of all their Energy. It was a dangerous power but one that could easily change the outcome of fights if they were skilled enough with the form.

Before long, the niyan that once stood in front of the assassin had transformed into a large black bear. After its transformation, it stood up and roared across the room, echoing off the walls.

Jacqueline jumped towards the beast and began her assault but was quickly swatted back into the nearby shelf. The books on the shelf toppled onto the floor, with some of the books falling onto her head.

She quickly rebounded and rushed at the beast once again, this time moving faster. As the bear swatted at Jacqueline, it would miss, causing more books to fall on them. Then, the adventurer pulled out a scroll from her pocket.

"Replo!"

Suddenly, the single Jacqueline duplicated into three. At different intervals, they would assault the bear. With each strike, the bear would roar in pain, attempting to counter-attack. It was, eventually, able to hit one of the clones, causing it to phase in and out of existence before disappearing.

The bear roared, once more, and a small shockwave shook the interior of the library, sending the remaining books into all directions. Jacqueline's other clone was instantly destroyed, and she was sent flying towards the end of the aisle against a stone wall.

She quickly regained her composure and breath and rushed towards the niyan once more. With each swipe, the bear would roar in pain, flailing back as it attempted to counter the assassin and her strikes. However, Jacqueline was just too fast.

The bear was able to hit her twice, once on the stomach and once on her left leg, causing her to bleed onto her clothes and onto the floor. When she was hit, she grimaced for a moment and returned to the fight, knowing she had to end it quickly.

Eventually, the bear fell to its knees and fell to the ground. It began to glow a red light before their body slowly returning to its original state. As the niyan remained face-down, naked, Jacqueline went over to them and placed two fingers onto their neck, checking for a pulse.

Their body was severely cut, bruised, and gashed. Blood had covered most of their body, seeping onto the floor underneath them. Still, Jacqueline kept searching for a pulse and was soon able to sense a very faint one.

She reached into her scroll bag and grabbed the healing scroll she had often used. After unravelling it, the scroll was placed onto the body of the niyan, covering their backside.

"Heal!"

A very light-yellow glow appeared from within the scroll and transferred into the niyan. The niyans' body emanated the yellow color, slowly taking them over. Their wounds, cuts, and bruises slowly started to fade, only leaving a scar in the worst of cases.

After the light-yellow light vanished, Jacqueline placed the fingers on her opponent once more. The pulse was more noticeable this time. Luckily for them, Jacqueline wasn't trying too hard to kill them. Her intention was to force them out of their spirit form, not kill them.

Now, she just had to wait.

CHAPTER IV

Sacrilege had long since set before Jacqueline's enemy woke from their slumber. As they came to, Zane noticed that his body was covered in a tattered white sheet, with their extremities latched to a long wooden allaic table they were resting on. For a moment or two, the niyan attempted to move his limbs—but to no avail.

Jacqueline was sitting in the corner, patiently waiting for him to get up. When she finally saw the niyan move, Jacqueline slowly got up and approached her attacker. She looked down at the niyan with a look of confusion and anger.

"Wh-where am I?" Zane asked, confused.

The room was a small room a floor or two underneath the large library. It was comprised of only the allaic table, several broken chairs, and a dimly lit lantern at the entrance. Cobwebs, the occasional spider, and the remains of other pests littered the room, telling the young assassin that it had not been touched in a fortnight.

"Ja-Jacquelinc!?" Zane yelled out, excited but also confused. "Where am I?"

"You don't know?" she answered, squinting her eyes as she attempted to see through his possible deception.

The niyan shook their head and attempted to move their arms and legs once again. With his eyes fully open, he noticed that his limbs had a leather strap around them that was bolted into the table. The niyan attempted to fight the binds for a moment or two more, only for his movements to become more frantic with each passing moment.

"Jacqueline!?" the niyan screamed out. "What are you doing to me!? What did I do to deserve this!?"

"You attacked me, Zane."

The niyan stopped what they were doing. They looked straight ahead for some time before moving their gaze towards Jacqueline's. His eyes were full of tears, confusion, and sadness, contrasting Jacqueline's serious, dark, focused demeanor.

When the two were younger, they would often get into trouble with their parents about going on adventures. Ethreos—the country they both hailed from—was a neutral territory in the global war for dominance. However, that did not mean the country was never left alone. All too often, the children of the country would be taken—in broad daylight or in the middle of the darkened night—to be used.

Jacqueline had lost count of how many times she and Zane were almost taken.

"*I* attacked *you*?" he sobbed.

Jacqueline nodded once.

A long silence befell the room for some time, with Zane looking straight ahead and sobbing occasionally. Jacqueline stayed silent, slowly walking around the room as she stared at the niyan from the corner of her eyes.

"I couldn't 've," he said, nearly whispering. "I'm... Not strong... You know this."

Jacqueline moved closer to the niyan, pointing towards her stomach and leg. After a moment, Zane looked up to see the dry gashes across the assassin's body, along with chunks of her armor missing. The niyan's eyes grew as they began to shake their head more.

"I couldn't 've!" he repeated. "I couldn't 've!"

"But, you did," Jacqueline responded, pulling out one of her daggers. "And you are going to tell me *who* sent you."

The niyan began to sob uncontrollably, so much so it began to hurt Jacqueline's ears as he screeched. While the room was far underneath the library, she began to worry if anyone would hear their shrieks for help.

"Quiet the fuck down," she ordered, placing their dagger against their throat a little harder.

Jacqueline, deep down, felt horrible about what she was doing. The two had been best friends since birth, with Jacqueline often seeing the niyan as the brother she never had, but she had to get to the bottom of this. It wasn't in

Zane's personality to attack anyone—let alone her—without provoke.

For now, she had to cast away her feelings if she wanted to find out who did this to her friend. And, once she found out, she would make sure they paid the price.

Zane stopped completely after the threat and began to hyperventilate. His eyes started to dart across the room at a high rate, and Jacqueline could feel his heart rate rising.

"Wh-wha-what's going on, Ja-Ja-Jacqueline?" he stuttered between sobs, attempting to control his breathing.

Jacqueline took her daggers off the niyan's throat, staring directly at him. Jacqueline could often tell if someone was lying to her, but it seemed like her friend was telling the truth. He was never this good of a liar, anyway. That was an unfortunate side-effect of being a loyal, trusting person like Zane—he couldn't lie like this.

"What was the last thing you remember?" she asked.

Zane took several deep breaths to recompose himself before resting his head against the table. There was a deep silence for several minutes as the niyan began to think things over slowly. Jacqueline waited patiently.

There were several moments that Jacqueline had to check to ensure he was still awake. The entire time Jacqueline saw him, he could see his eyes darting back and forth slowly as if reading something off a page. Was he just in deep thought?

"I remember… Being in my bed," he began. "My bed… Home, in Ethreos. Uh, there was a tornado outside causing so much… So much destruction. The winds were loud; it felt as if my home would fly away any moment."

His words started to trail off, leaving a few moments of silence for Jacqueline to interject.

"Etheros never has tornadoes—was this magical in nature?"

Even if one was not entuned with spellcraft, it wasn't too difficult to determine if a disaster was manmade. Natural disasters were spawns of nature herself, created randomly through the world—their patterns nearly impossible to determine. Manmade disasters—on the other hand—required an extreme amount of Energy, so much so it often left the user Energy-sickened for weeks on end. To add to this, manmade disasters were imperfect and often radiated a strong magical aura that could be sensed for miles, even by non-spellcasters.

"Ye-yeah, I think it was," Zane said, his words once again trailing off.

"How destroyed is your home, now?"

Zane took another moment to ponder the question.

"It… Came straight for me," he finally said.

Jacqueline leaned against the wall, looking straight down as she began to think things through. While it was obvious someone was coming for her, why would they choose Zane of all people? Why not someone much stronger, like Max Alam? It just didn't make sense.

While still deep in thought, Jacqueline walked over and slashed open the leather straps with one swift move. Now free from his confines, Zane got up and eyed his friend. It wasn't like Jacqueline to be this confused—she was one of the sharpest women he knew.

"Jack?" asked Zane.

Jacqueline didn't answer. Either she was ignoring Zane for calling her Jack, or she was in much deeper thought than he had imagined. Either way, it was very much unlike her.

"Jacqueline?" Zane called out again.

"Do you... Do you know the story of the Lich of Izaman?"

CHAPTER V

The rest of the evening was spent by both Zane and Jacqueline as they fixed the library. Toppled shelves were raised back up one-by-one, with their books placed back neatly on them. Some of the books suffered major damages, with some of their covers deteriorating further from the showdown.

The two of them were silent as the library was rebuilt. Once they came up from the basement levels, not a word had been muttered by the two. Jacqueline was still deep in thought as she attempted to determine her true enemy, and Zane was thinking over the story that the assassin had told him so far.

By the time Sacrilege began to show the first light of the day, most of the damage was already fixed. All that remained were torn pages, spell marks, and the occasional small puddle of blood.

"Eh," Jacqueline said out-loud, for the first time in many hours. "It adds character."

Zane chuckled slightly as he worked on cleaning up as much blood as he could. He soon realized that his method was only making things worse with the blood being smeared further into the ground. After he was done, he threw the wool rag into a small container they had found and threw it outside with the rest of the garbage.

"Morning, already?" groaned Zane as he saw Sacrilege poke out from the western horizon.

Jacqueline didn't respond, already refocusing her attention on what to do next. While the trek to Zala proved fruitful, it also raised even more questions that she had to answer.

Jacqueline picked up the tome given to her by the Seer and the previously locked book—*The Tomb of the Lich*—and began to walk towards the entrance of the library. The more she walked, the more the light returned to the library, illuminating the darkness. As she continued to think, the assassin didn't hear someone run up behind her.

At least she had the map to the tomb and, now, she can begin to stop Meredith's resurrection. If she rested for the day, she and Ramadier could be there by the end of the week. At least, that is what she had hoped.

Still, she knew it might not end well; she still knew little about the tomb itself, or if it was still trapped or enchanted. There was no way the tomb was placed with no magical or physical traps protecting it.

"Wait!"

She stopped at the entrance of the library, hearing the voice of Zane from not far behind her. She turned around to see that the niyan—just like when they were younger—was not too far behind her, just like her shadow.

"Where're you going?" he asked.

Jacqueline held up *The Tomb of the Lich*. The niyan stared at the book for a moment and then nodded his head.

"The least I could do is help you."

"No."

"Wh-why not!?"

"You'll just get in the way."

It was a harsh thing to say, yes, but Jacqueline didn't want Zane more involved then he was already. If someone went to great lengths to brainwash the niyan and bring him to Zalzabar in hopes of thwarting her plans on stopping Meredith, there was no telling what could happen next.

Jacqueline turned around and started to step outside, only to be stopped by someone pulling on her hand. By reaction, she twisted around and nearly punched Zane in the jaw, stopping mere inches from his face. Zane didn't flinch.

"I'm coming with you, whether you like it or not."

Jacqueline sighed heavily then rubbed her face. If anything, she was far too tired to argue.

"Fine, but I'm calling the shots."

———

It was almost dusk when Jacqueline awoke from her sleep. She groaned when she realized that the entire day was spent sleeping, which meant there was less time to get to the tomb. The adventurer quickly jumped up and grabbed both of her books—one from the Seer, the other from the library—and began to read them more. Zane, unsurprisingly, was still sleeping in the adjacent room, which gave her some time to read. While the idea of leaving without him crossed her mind, she had a suspicion that any help—even from someone like Zane—would be beneficial to her in the end.

The Tomb of the Lich continued to give no clear answers as to what awaited the two. She had hoped that the writer of the book would give more information, but there wasn't a lot useful besides the map. It only continued to frustrate her.

However, during her research, she was able to find a fascinating discovery: the cave paintings she saw before were explained, in full detail, as to what it meant. It retold the legend of Meredith, the Lich of Izaman, and her rise to power. Most of the details spoken by the Seer were repeated in the texts, but there were some details that weren't mentioned.

Meredith was a Child of Sin, the offspring of two different races—a human mother and a zichan father. Her mother, Ayla, and her father, Bishop, had a hidden romance for almost a decade before they decided to bear a child. After Meredith's birth, the two attempted to keep it hidden, but they were ultimately betrayed by one of their dearest friends.

In return for a vast amount of gold, the traitor turned in his friends. Ayla and Bishop were stoned and mocked by their former neighbors until they were burned to death for their ultimate sin.

Meredith witnessed the execution of her parents, watching as they cried in terror and cried in pain as those they once thought as friends betrayed them. Her heart, once of good and purity, began to darken. On that very fateful day, she vowed revenge.

By the age of twenty-two, Meredith had grown to a level that rivalled that of the oldest of mages. Fueled by the darkness in her heart, the ever-lasting screams of her parents crying for help, and pure anger and rage she had towards all of mortalkind, the soon-to-be Lich began to aim the denizens of Ethos.

The book continued to talk about the true power of Meredith in disturbing detail. As a trophy of her victories, she would rip out the heart of her still-living victim. Those who died to her were forced into her version of purgatory, being forced to feel their death over-and-over until the end of time.

Some of the details within the book also alluded to her being the first mortal to unlock her Gate—thus increasing her magical prowess to levels that rival the Old Gods. Other details spoke of how, with a flick of her wrist, half of a town could be destroyed in a massive explosion. The scarier details spoke of how she was learning how to harness her Energy to give her an immortal life; something never thought possible.

Eventually, by the time she was twenty-four, she had risen an undead army to destroy the world of Ethos. Her forces of the dead waged war on the countries of Ethos, with many falling to her in a matter of months. No one in the realm could defeat her.

That is, until the six legendary heroes known as the Omni joined forces to rid of her darkness forever. Not much is known about the Omni, not even the names of the chosen heroes are known. However, because of them, Meredith was ultimately slain. Her soul—too powerful to ever be destroyed—was imprisoned in another dimension, never to return. However, it seems like that was never meant to last, either.

All this information was fascinating to Jacqueline. During her travels around the world, she had met many spellcasters from all walks of life. All of them were powerful in their own ways, mastering one of the six elements to help better mortalkind. Still, they all paled in comparison for the darkness that was to come.

A darkness that was nearing its second coming.

"You done reading?"

Jacqueline snapped up from her book to see Zane standing above her. He was wearing light leather armor with steel woven around his joints and torso. On his belt, there were two short steel swords. It seems the niyan is ready.

"Yeah, for now," she responded, placing the book on the table.

"Are you going to get ready, then?"

Jacqueline rubbed her temples for a second, then nodded. She had gotten so engrossed into writing that she had forgotten to get ready. Sacrilege was already setting, and they desperately needed the veil of night. If an Order patrol found Zane, they would both be killed on the spot. Zane's presence only made the mission much more difficult.

Zane left Jacqueline's inn room, allowing her to strip out of her old bed garments. When she did so, Jacqueline peered at herself in the mirror, still seeing the scratches and gashes she attained from her fight with the niyan standing just outside her door. While she had some knowledge of healing her wounds, she hadn't found the time to do so. They were on limited time, right now.

She reached over for the rest of her undergarments and tunic, quickly putting them on. Once they were on, she quickly equipped her dark-blue leather armor, strapping it down to ensure it couldn't slip off her.

Jacqueline sheathed her two daggers into her belt and turned around to exit the room, where Zane was waiting. The niyan had his arms crossed as he looked up at the ceiling. Even after she exited the room, Zane didn't give her much attention.

"Ready," mentioned Jacqueline.

Zane nodded his head without looking over at the assassin and began to move towards the stairs. Jacqueline followed shortly after, double-checking herself to ensure she had all her gear for the journey ahead. There was no returning, at least until Meredith was defeated once more.

The bar of the inn was empty, an oddity for this time of night. It made things easier for them, as to not draw attention to the bear symbol upon Zane's forehead. While there were a few who secretly sympathized with the niyans, it was wise to assume everyone was with the Order.

A small bell rang as they exited the bar, not alarming anyone nearby. As they did so, they could see that the many moons of Ethos—all six of them—shone brightly in the night sky. From Sian to Araa, the moons often showed the inhabitants of Ethos what lay beyond their war-torn, broken world. However, even with the advances in teleportation, it proved an expensive endeavor to leave the world they learned to dislike.

The two walked over to the stables, to find both Ramadier and Ka—Zane's horse—waiting for them. Both horses had two or three bags already on them, filled with the food and supplies attained by Jacqueline earlier that day.

Jacqueline unlatched their gates and jumped onto Ramadier, taking his reins, and proceeded out of the stables. Zane soon followed, stopping right in front of Jacqueline. For a split moment, she began to inspect Ka and what they were. Ka was a beautiful horse, looking to be of a mix between mesia and another breed she knew not. The horse possessed a beautiful brown mane with white streaks going through it in a zig-zag pattern. There were also several dozen white spots across their body.

Jacqueline pulled out her map and began to look around. On her map, she placed the location of the Tomb of the Lich. If the book were to be believed, the tomb would be towards the center of Zalzabar in the Ila Mountains. It was probably one of the best places to hide the tomb, as the Ila Mountains were never known for their hospitable terrain.

The young assassin snapped the reins, pointed to the left—west—and began to run in that direction. The niyan soon followed, keeping speed with the speedy pure-blooded mesia in front of them.

"We haven't spoken in a few years," Jacqueline said as the two sat next to the warm fire.

Zalzabar was not known for its kind weather, oftentimes becoming a winter tundra overnight in the winter months. During the summer months, it was the opposite with the sun drowning the land in its warm light. Also adding to the heat was the extreme humidity the country could face.

Fortunately, even with Jacqueline's limited spellcraft ability, she could create a small campfire. The flame crackled and spat into the air, breaking the near silence that befell the two for quite some time.

"Four years, to be exact," Zane returned.

Zane had a long black cloak wrapped around him in a vain attempt to stay warm. The cloak was made of a fine linen that was almost too thin to protect against the elements.

The niyan took several sips from his warm teacup, before placing it back on the small plate it came with. Even though the handle of the cup was cold, he still acted as if it were by pinching the handle.

"How have things been?" asked Jacqueline. "Did you get anywhere with…?"

Zane shook his head, as Jacqueline's words began to trail off. The niyan placed his cup of tea onto the plate and placed it to the side. He rubbed his face several times, then gazed up at the stars above.

"I could never find her," he said after a moment's break.

Kendra... Jacqueline thought to herself.

While the two were once inseparable, there was a third person within their group; that person being Kendra, Zane's twin sister. From what Jacqueline could remember, Kendra was always the more courageous of the two, showing the most promise in combat, and even possessed the spirt animal of a dragon—a rarity in this day and age. However, four years ago, Kendra mysteriously vanished. Thinking the Order was behind it, Zane began on a quest to figure out where his sister was and save her.

It seems like his quest was far from over.

"The last I heard," said the niyan, breaking the silence once more. "She was heading to Arcanus to meet the Bandit King, but that was a year ago. The trail goes cold after that."

Instantly, Jacqueline began to question the legitimacy of what Zane just said. The Bandit King, Tao, was never one to be trifled with; this was the same man who stormed Arcanus, the most powerful nation in the North Star Alliance and brought it to its knees in no time. No one in their right mind would consider talking to him.

That is unless they had a strong bargaining chip.

"What did she have to offer him?"

Zane shook his head. It seemed as if not even he was able to answer that part of the puzzle.

"What've you been doing the past four years?" he asked, trying to change the subject.

What haven't I done?

Jacqueline let a smile slip past her lips before she looked down to the ground to hide it. Not to let the question fall on deaf ears, she began to slowly formulate an answer; but where to start? For the past four years, ever since she was seventeen, she had been adventuring.

If anything, the past four years were all but a blur to her. When you adventured around Ethos—and even Sian—as much as she had, you tend to lose track of time. There were, of course, several moments that defined her career as an adventurer and as a hero, but she tended to not dwell on them for long. Often those who reminisced about the past were often the ones ill-suited for the tasks at hand.

"Have you ever heard of the Great Wyrm?" she asked after some time.

"No, I haven't," Zane replied, shaking his head.

"Do you at least know what wyrms are?"

Zane shook his head no. It was normal—most mortals in today's world never read into the planet's long, dark history. The wyrms were one such species caught up in the endless struggle for control of Ethos. And, for that, they were pushed to near extinction.

"Long ago," began the assassin. "The wyrms—a powerful species devolved from the dragons—fought side-by-side with the mortal races. They were—and still are—a beautiful species that commanded respect to the raw intelligence. However, three hundred years ago, the Great Hunt began... And millions were slaughtered."

Zane looked down at the fire, not sure how to respond. The two sat in silence for some time before the niyan spoke up.

"W-why?"

"Their horns commanded a high price," Jacqueline responding whilst shaking her head.

"What does the Great Wyrm have to do with this, then?"

"The Great Wyrm is their protector, guarding the entrance to their home in the darkness below. On occasion, they would venture to the surface and attack anyone nearby; not only to protect their home but as revenge."

"And... I am guessing you were tasked to kill them?"

Jacqueline shook her head once.

"Not just me, though," she mentioned. "There were three others: Xavier the Unfortunate, Amalia Ocaron, and Max Alam. All four of us ventured to the entrance. However only Max and I was able to escape alive."

"I… I'm sorry."

"I still hear their screams... And their cries. I can still see their mangled bodies scattered across the floor, begging to be put out of their misery. I can… I can see the bloody stare they gave me as they gave their last breath."

Jacqueline started to shiver. In all the years Zane knew her, he had never seen Jacqueline this vulnerable. Jacqueline was always the one who was strong, confident, and motivated; now she was the opposite of it. Whoever this wyrm was, they were not to be trifled with.

Zane looked up at the sky to see the moons hovering above them. He stared at the majesty of the six moons for some time before he returned to meet Jacqueline's gaze.

"The past is the past," he said courageously. "What was done cannot be undone, but the future is still waiting to be written."

Jacqueline gave a small smile as she continued to stare at her friend. She used to say that phrase when the two were younger.

The future awaits.

CHAPTER VI

Several days had passed before the two arrived at where the tomb was said to be. Ever since the night by the fire, the two hardly spoke to one another as they started to mentally prepare themselves for the trials that laid ahead.

Jacqueline had read over both the tome and book several times during their trip but was sure she could not gather any more information. She concluded that the Tomb of the Lich was created before Meredith defeated, meaning that any traps laid after her entombment would not be in the books. The two would have to be extra cautious when they entered the tomb, even more so then before; they were entering blind.

The tomb was deep within the Ila Mountain range. The two had arrived at the range a day or two before but spent the rest of the time checking, double checking, and triple checking the map and clues for the exact location of the tomb. By the time they had discovered it in the snowiest parts of the mountains, most of their supplies had been lost and their food eaten.

The entrance of the tomb was made of black stone, most of which covered in snow and ice. Jacqueline, sparingly, used several fire spells to show the dark temple in its entirety. As they cautiously walked up the steps, they could see a heavily rusted iron door ahead of them.

With little effort, the two were able to knock the door down. Ahead of them were more icy steps leading down into darkness. Jacqueline took the lead and summoned two small lights to illuminate the path ahead of them.

It took some time for both Jacqueline and Zane to traverse the dangerous steps into the tomb. With the tomb being over a thousand years old, was bound to have a substantial number of pitfalls and eroded steps.

The steps into the tomb were littered with bones, ash, and vermin. As their lights shone the path forward, the vermin scattered back into the endless darkness. The pattering of their feet could be heard as the pair descended further into the darkness. Eventually, they were met with a large stone room that spiralled against the wall further downwards.

The stairs were long and treacherous, with a large portion of the stone steps appearing to be missing. To continue further down, the two had to make large leaps across the chasms, praying the stone they would land on would not give.

At one point, Zane picked up a large boulder and threw it into the endless abyss beneath them. Even with his more sensitive hearing, he could not hear the enormous rock hit the ground below.

When he never heard the rock, Zane's heart skipped a beat and a drop of sweat could be felt going down his face. Doubt—and even regret—began to overtake him, causing him to wonder if he should retreat from the adventure altogether. He volunteered for this journey, and he wishes he didn't.

Jacqueline continued the conquest to the ground floor with a certain focus that Zane had never seen before. When they were younger, Jacqueline, while courageous, was often headstrong and unfocused in what she wanted to do. Because of this, she would often get into trouble when she broke to covenants she was bound to follow by the elders of their hometown.

Now, it was obvious to Zane that she had grown up. While she had her moments of weakness—like by the fire days prior—Zane knew she hadn't changed. She was stronger, more skilful, more confident, and more ambitious about her quests. In many ways, he admired his friend; he wish he could become the same.

Jacqueline held her hand up, balling it into a fist. Zane recognized the gesture, ceasing his movement immediately. Silence befell the area, with only the shifting of rocks and dirt being the only sound their minds could focus on.

The assassin began to look around, patiently, as she began to look around. At one point, she looked down at the step she was standing on, only seeing a pile of rubble and dirt underneath her.

As suddenly as she stopped, she began to move forward again, with Zane following. He had known her long enough to know that she sensed something; there was no point in questioning her.

Assassins, often, knew when a trap was imminent. Usually, there was some sign pointing to the likelihood of a trap—an out of place object, a sudden sound change, or even a "gut feeling." Jacqueline was no different; if she felt like they needed to stop, it was for a valid reason.

As the pair continued to descend the rough stone stairs, Zane threw several more rocks to the bottom, eventually hearing them hit the ground below. After what felt like hours, at long last, they were close to returning to a solid, reliable ground.

Jacqueline quickly cast a light down to the bottom. The light, eventually, stopped and hovered over the center of the spiralling staircase. Part of her wanted to jump from where she was and allow her reflexes to prevent her from taking a substantial amount of damage from hitting the stone ground. But, she also felt as if the ground below was trapped. Until now, the fabled tomb of the most powerful necromancer in existence had zero traps to prevent graverobbers. Something was amiss.

Zane was the first to touch the ground floor, jumping several feet ahead of Jacqueline. When he did so, he took a deep breath and sat down, exhausted from the long descension. Jacqueline followed suit, taking a few drinks from her canteen as they recovered from their trek.

Suddenly, their light went out.

"Lightoa!" commanded Jacqueline.

Nothing happened.

"What in the Hells?"

"Lightoa!" repeated Zane.

Again, nothing happened.

The darkness was overwhelming, absorbing all light in the area. Each time Jacqueline or Zane commanded a light spell, they could feel a small part of their Energy waste away, but there was nothing to appear.

"Jacqueline?" asked Zane. "What do we do?"

Jacqueline hesitated. Was this a trap? Had they unknowingly triggered something that absorbed all the light they could summon? If that were the case, what else was there to worry about? It was unlikely this was the only trap.

Her armor shimmied as Jacqueline rose from her spot on the ground. She unsheathed both her daggers and looked forward, as least she hoped it was forward. Behind her, she could hear Zane do the same, wielding both of his longswords.

"Do we have a rope?" she asked.

"Yeah," Zane replied.

While Jacqueline could not see it, she knew the niyan was reaching into one of his bags. Eventually, he was able to feel a rope inside of the bag and pulled it out. Quickly, he tied the rope around his waist, then handed Jacqueline the other end.

Jacqueline tied the rope tightly around her waist, then pulled slightly on it. Zane simply replied saying it was secure, giving the adventurer permission to walk forward.

For a moment, Zane hesitated before moving forward with Jacqueline. Anxiety had paralyzed him the fear of the unknown had clouded his ability to think clearly.

Jacqueline reached behind her, pushing the palm of her hand into Zane's chest. The niyan, startled, let out a gasp before remaining quiet. Just as before, the area around them was quiet. Zane's hairs started to extend on end as anxiety quickly clouded him again.

"Move right!" Jacqueline yelled out.

Immediately, the pair jumped to the right. While doing so, a large blade swished past them, clashing to the stone floor below them. A wet shriek filled the air around them as the assailant picked up the blade once more.

Another slash quickly came for Jacqueline, this time causing the assassin to block the attack. Even with her inability to see, she was able to hear where and in which direction a blade was coming from. However, she underestimated their speed, almost missing her block entirely.

Their opponent shrieked once more as they slashed at Jacqueline several more times, each time being blocked successfully. With each attack, Jacqueline was beginning to understand their patterns to find an opening. Even though their enemy had a fast and sporadic pattern of attack, it was only a matter of time before she figured them out.

With another downward slash, she was able to parry the attack, then plunged both of her daggers forward. She could feel the blades cut through a rough flesh, eventually cutting deeper into their skin. Upon impact, the creature shrieked a terrible shriek that rivalled that of Nightmares.

Jacqueline continued her assault, taking more swipes and slashes at their adversary. Each swipe was met with another scream that echoed across the walls. Her fury only continued as the shrieking continued to get more and more silent. Once the creature was silent, and it had fallen to the stone floor below, Jacqueline plunged her daggers one last time into them.

This time, nothing.

Jacqueline, after withdrawing her bloodied blades, stood back and began to breathe heavily. Adrenaline had taken control of her body in the short conflict, allowing her to achieve victory in the face of an advantageous opponent.

"You alright!?" yelled Zane into the darkness.

"Y-yeah," Jacqueline responded, still breathing heavy.

Right as Jacqueline kneeled to the ground below, a loud shriek could be heard in front of her. A red light illuminated the room for a moment, allowing for both Zane and Jacqueline to assess the situation. During that one moment, Jacqueline was able to see that the shrieking was coming from the creature she had just slain. The creature was humanoid in many aspects. However, it possessed four large arms and two heads. The creature's skin was made out scales, like that of a snake. However, between the scales, a purple ooze could be seen pouring out of them.

The purple ooze had a profuse odor to it that caused both Zane and Jacqueline to gag for a few moments. It smelled of rotten, cooked eggs, but even worse than that somehow. It was the kind of stench that, if around for even moments, it would seep into your pores, making it difficult to remove.

Jacqueline jumped back to her feet, then slashed at the rope keeping her and Zane joined.

"Zane, run!" ordered Jacqueline.

"What!? Why!? Where!?" he yelled back.

"Do as I say! This is a rellagate!"

"A fucking what!?"

Zane cursed once more then turned to run to where they descended from. The red light has long since passed, but he was still able to feel the walls leading back to the base of the stairs, leaving Jacqueline to her fight with whatever a rellagate was.

The rellagate shrieked once more, then began to rise to its feet. While it was doing so, a red aura swirled around the monster until it eventually returned to its normal fighting stance. Once the red aura had disappeared, the room's darkness returned once more, blinding Jacqueline from seeing once more.

Suddenly, Jacqueline heard two separate slashes come for her, from two completely different angles. She reacted quickly, blocking both attacks with the handguard of her daggers. She was able to win the battle of strength, pushing the creature back until it returned soon after to continue their assault.

With each slash, Jacqueline attempted to block as best as she could. Even with her speed and endurance, it was proving difficult to keep up with the creature as the battle dragged on. When it was not possible for her to block, she dodged and weaved through the attacks as best as she could. The rellagate's blades came towards her faster and faster. She knew, eventually, she had to switch to an offensive stance.

Then, the rellagate was able to disarm Jacqueline by flinging her dagger to the side. The dagger bounced across the stone floor before stopping behind Jacqueline, but she was unable to reach for it with the relentless assault of the reptile creature in front of her.

She was able to block several more attacks before she was kicked to the ground by the large reptile. The monster's hissing grew louder as it approached her.

As Jacqueline was attempting to stand back up, she heard a large thumping sound rush from the side. Thinking it was another opponent, she began to count her blessings, knowing she could not take on two enemies in the darkness. This might be it for her.

Instead, she was met with a loud shrieking noise from the rellagate. Then, she heard the roar of a bear as it attacked. There was only one bear she knew here.

"Zane!" yelled out Jacqueline.

While she could not see, she could hear the shrieks and yells of the rellagate as it continued to fight the bear. It was impossible for Jacqueline to know who was winning the confrontation, but she eventually heard the rellagate's cries grow more and more silent as Zane's roars grew louder.

"Lightoa!"

A magical light appeared and blinded Jacqueline, forcing her to hold up her hands in a desperate attempt to block it.

With the defeat of the rellagate, light was able to return to the area around them. When her vision slowly returned, she could see the mangled remains of the rellagate—its limbs were ripped from its sockets entirely, with a gush of blood and purple ooze having soaked the stone floor. As Jacqueline looked around, she could see most of the floor coated in the purple, foul ooze. When she searched around for Zane, she eventually found him in the corner, bleeding profusely.

"Zane!" she cried out, reaching into her bag for her healing spells. It took some time for her to find the heal spell—the same she had used previously—but she soon placed it on the wounded bear's stomach.

"Otomo shalador!"

A magical white light soon appeared, transferring and overtaking the bear's body. As time went on, the blood ceased to pour of their wounds and the wounds closed. During this time, the bear started to grow smaller until he returned to his previous niyan state.

The wounds on Zane had disappeared entirely, but there were still many scars across his body. Jacqueline, hesitantly, placed her fingers on his throat, searching for a pulse. To her surprise, there was a strong pulse coming from the niyan; she was expecting it to be faint. It seemed like Zane, her savior, had collapsed from a lack of Energy.

As Jacqueline looked on to her friend, she heard a shriek to her right. Without a second thought, she took the tip of her remaining dagger and threw it into the direction of the rellagate. Once more, the shrieks went silent.

After it halted, Jacqueline looked over to see a red aura still surrounding the monster. She rose to her feet, balled her fists, and assumed her combat stance, ready to fight whatever was to come next. Whatever this creature was, it was proving difficult to finally end.

Thoughts of the rellagate being afflicted with Meredith's necromancy went through Jacqueline's mind. She had read about fighting undead creatures, but she had no idea how to finally stop them. Were they truly eternal creatures?

As the thoughts continued to pour in, the red aura manifesting around the rellagate started to float above their body. Before long, the aura had turned itself into a humanoid shape. Two piercing yellow eyes suddenly appeared from the red, staring straight at the assassin in front of them. Jacqueline, as courageous as ever, looked back at them.

"Okawa, huam ata'ach?"

Jacqueline squinted. She knew from her time with the Sixth Signet that the… Thing in front of her was speaking Atrian, or at least some form of it. However, she could not place what they were saying.

"Okawa, huam ata'ach?" they repeated.

"Kria okawa at'em," she responded. "I do not speak Atrian."

That was, more or less, all Jacqueline knew of the nearly forgotten language.

"Then, so be it," the voice responded. *"Do you not know of this place, bringer of light, bringer of salvation?"*

Jacqueline looked over to see that one of her daggers was to the left of her, with the other dagger still in the forehead of the rellagate she just fought. It was good to keep track of her weapons, just in case this got ugly.

"Answer me!" the voice demanded.

The room's color shifted between red and yellow several times before it settled down once more.

Jacqueline spat on the ground in front of her in response to the dark voice.

"I do. What of it?"

The yellow eyes squinted towards Jacqueline, then a hiss could be heard from all directions.

"You mortals are all the same; weak, feeble, pathetic. You dare *enter the tomb of a Goddess!?"*

"I'm sorry, who are you?"

The red aura slowly hovered over to Jacqueline, slowly transforming into a more recognizable shape. From the bottom of their foot to the top of their head, the features of their body became more detailed. Before long, a beautiful woman stood in front of Jacqueline.

The woman had long red hair, with the same yellow eyes from before. The complexion of the woman made her seem younger—much younger than Jacqueline in fact. Her pointed, zichan ears were pierced with large ruby stones that bore the symbol of fire. She wore a long red dress that extended from just above her cleavage to the floor below. On each of her hands, she wore a similarly red glove with the Majic symbol of darkness on the back of them.

"Do you recognize me, now?" she asked, staring at the assassin.

The stare was intimidating. The Energy surrounding the room was active, swirling around them both at a high rate. It was so fast, in fact, that it stung Jacqueline's body. However, she couldn't show a moment of weakness to the necromancer.

"Can't say I do."

The woman snarled at what Jacqueline said and looked over at the mangled corpse of the rellagate. She pointed to the creature for a moment, and a black ray extended from the tip of her fingers into the creature. Slowly, the mangled corpse began to come back together and reform into the rellagate they had previously fought. It soon began to rise, shrieking for just a moment. Then, the spellcaster held out another finger, forcing the rellagate to painfully disintegrate into ash. All that could be heard were the cries and shrieks before their ashes fell to the ground below.

"This is your last chance to flee, mortal," the necromancer threatened. *"Continue, and you will suffer a similar fate to my disciple."*

Jacqueline hardly flinched while the necromancer was performing her ungodly acts. Inside, she could feel her fear starting to grow; never has she seen a powerful spellcaster like the Lich before.

The necromancer gave a small smirk, bearing her fangs to the adventurer. She chuckled for a moment then began to float back to where the rellagate once stood.

Was it possible Meredith could feel Jacqueline's fear?

"My resurrection nears, mortal," gloated the necromancer. *"Soon, the light shall fade once more, and the world shall suffer for my imprisonment. Soon, the shadows shall envelop the world, casting this godless realm into eternal damnation!"*

"Not if we stop you, first."

The Lich looked to the side of the room, towards the base of the stairs. Jacqueline's gaze followed her, meeting the eyes of an uncovered niyan approaching them. Zane was breathing heavily and limping towards them, one of his hands placed on his ribs.

Seeing this, all the Lich could do was laugh. Her laugh—one of pure madness and evil—reverbed off the walls, echoing lightly inside of the tall, spiraling room. Then, the necromancer returned her yellow eyes to the niyan.

"A niyan?" she laughed. *"An offspring of the First Sin has come to stop an immortal? Your fathers and father's fathers are why the Gods left. Your ancestors are what gave* me *strength!"*

Zane took another few steps forward, gripping onto his sword tighter as he approached the spirit in front of them. Jacqueline could see an intense anger, an intense fire, start to build. As he took more steps forward, his breathing started to settle, and his limping ceased.

"You know not of my ancestors, witch!" he roared out.

The Lich smirked again, keeping her gaze on the niyan. Suddenly, her spirit began to fade in front of the two. She returned her eyes towards Jacqueline who had not moved a muscle during the interaction.

"If you mortals wish to challenge a Goddess," Meredith threatened. *"Find me... And suffer."*

Her spirit completely faded, but not before Zane rushed over and slashed his blades at where the spirit once was. The force of the blades was so strong, some of the rellagate's ashes flew away.

"Dammit!" cursed out the niyan, throwing his swords to the ground.

Jacqueline walked over to her friend, who had his head in his hands. She could hear a very faint sob coming from the niyan—a sob of frustration.

"We'll find her," she assured. "But, first, you need to rest."

CHAPTER VII

There was a deep silence for several hours as the two settled around the small light Jacqueline had summoned. In fear of the toxic fumes around them, they refused to start a fire inside the confines of the tomb. Instead, the light was all they had to prevent the permanent darkness from returning.

Jacqueline was able to makeshift some cloth from the torn pieces of clothes when Zane transformed, making it easier for her to look at him without feeling awkward. Even then, the niyan was topless, but at least he wasn't bottomless.

There was still a plentiful amount of food available in the bags, allowing the pair to rest before they continued trek into the tomb. For Zane, he had several apples placed next to him; although he had yet to eat any of them. For the assassin, however, she only had a banana; she wasn't too hungry.

"What is the First Sin?" asked Jacqueline suddenly.

She had heard of the concept in the past, but it felt like every historian had their own definition or idea of what it was. For many, it was the reason the Gods left the realm to begin with due to some worshipping false deities. For others, it was the idea that all mortalkind had forgotten the Gods entirely.

"For the niyans," began Zane. "It is the source of all of our sorrow, all of our hate, all of our despair… And all our past, present, and future."

Jacqueline tilted her head, not wanting to interrupt. As Zane continued to speak, his voice grew softer and softer, as if he were retreating inward. There was another silence before the niyan continued.

"Long ago, there were six beings of purity," he continued. "These beings—the Omni was what my people called them—were the perfect disciples of the Gods. In a way, they were like the Seers and Priests of our time, being the truest of believers to the Gods. The Omni represented each of the six elements—fire, water, earth, wind, light, and dark."

Zane started to draw in the ashes of the rellagate next to him, creating six circles. Then, he connected each of the six circles together in a mesh, akin to how old texts often depicted them.

"The Omni were powerful beings, able to perform miracles in the name of their masters. They were to keep balance in the world, ensuring we all lived in harmony. The leader of the Omni was a niyan known as Erakai—whose element was darkness.

"However, all of that changed one day. At the end of the Fourth Era, he was influenced by a greater power—the truest of all evils, and the source of the shadows themselves.

Erakai betrayed and murdered the other Omni, sending the world into despair. The Gods saw this, from beginning to end, and left, knowing the true potential of the mortal races. For if the Omni were influenced by Sato, anyone could be."

As he spoke, Zane quickly brushed through the ashes, erasing what he had drew. Then, he picked up a handful, rose it into the air, and let it trickle out of his hands, forming a mountain in the floor.

"What happened to Erakai?" asked Jacqueline.

Zane shook his head.

"No one knows," he answered. "Erakai disappeared, along with the Majic and the Gods. With no one else to answer for the crimes of one dark person, my race answered for it. Now, over a thousand years later… We are nearly extinct. Murder. Genocide. Prejudice. Those are the first words we learn as infants."

"The First Wish," Jacqueline muttered.

Zane nodded his head once.

"The very Wish that destroyed my race; within moments of it being granted, millions died and the left were eternally weakened. Now, it is rare for a niyan to bear a child."

Jacqueline struggled to figure out how to change the subject. She would be the first to admit she was ignorant to history, only knowing what had happened in recent years. But, she also knew the questions were hurting Zane's spirit;

one can only be hated for so long before you begin to believe those around you.

Instead, she knew it was time they continued. Even though Zane had only a few hours rest—it often took days for one to recover the Energy expelled from transforming—it was time to continue. Meredith was growing in strength with each passing moment.

Jacqueline reached over into her bag, pulling out the book she retrieved from the library. She quickly sifted through the pages in a vain search of information on what was to come next. While there were brief mentions about what traps awaited inside of the tomb, they never detailed where they were placed.

The traps she was able to read about ranged from the normal spike and arrow traps to more elaborate ones, such as fake floors. She didn't have time to study what the traps were; she just wanted to know what was ahead. However, the book continued to provide nothing.

"What next?" asked the niyan.

Jacqueline peered up and met Zane's gaze.

"We have to move," she answered.

Zane nodded and stood up slowly, almost falling back over. Jacqueline reached over to help the niyan, but he refused to take it. Instead, he gripped his twin blades and began to move towards an archway behind them.

Jacqueline grabbed her things and followed the niyan towards the archway. She ran in front of him enough to where only she could trigger traps so that he would hopefully stay safe.

"You should head back, Zane," she said.

"No," he answered.

There was no arguing with him, and Jacqueline knew that. Even when they were younger, Zane was never one to take orders or commands, even if they were in the right—it just who he was. In a way, Jacqueline commended the courage he had acquired in the years since, but she knew that Zane could be walking right into his death. He could barely walk, let alone withstand the assault of an all-powerful mage.

Still, Zane kept up to the assassin as best as he could. Jacqueline tried to keep ahead as much as she could, acting as a layer of protection for him, but he would often catch up to her.

The hallway they walked down was small and claustrophobic. The stone walls and ceiling were closed in, ensuring their movement was limited. Because of this, Jacqueline had the suspicion that there was a trap within this hall, but she had yet to find it.

As she led, Jacqueline scanned the walls, floor, and ceiling ahead of her to check for possible holes or cracks. The stone, instead, was in near pristine condition, as if it were laid out recently. While this made it easier for her to spot possible issues, it gave her an unsettling feeling.

What was more unsettling was how far they had walked with no exit or possible traps. It felt like the two had been walking for a while, with no clear change.

Out of intuition, Jacqueline grabbed one of her daggers and quickly slashed both sides of the wall before returning them to her belt. Zane jumped back slightly at the sudden move and looked back at the cuts in the wall as they continued forward.

"Wh-what was that about?" he asked.

"You'll see," she answered, not saying any more.

Zane's eyebrows rose slightly at the comment, then shook his head. Sometimes, with Jacqueline, there wasn't much rhyme or reason to things. All he could do was wait it out and see the results.

Some time passed, then Jacqueline stopped in her tracks. Zane stopped behind her, and before he could ask why they stopped, Jacqueline pointed to the wall. On the wall, there was a single slash, with another slash on the other wall.

"Oh," Zane blurted out. "The hallway is repeating?"

"It seems like it," Jacqueline answered.

While they were walking down the hallway, she could not find a single hole, crack, or imperfection in the walls surrounding them. There was something she was missing, but Jacqueline could not figure out what.

"What if…?" asked Zane before his question trailed off.

Jacqueline looked behind her to see Zane rubbing his hand against the wall. Before she had a chance to ask for him to continue, Zane did.

"What if there is an imaginary wall somewhere?"

"That's it!" Jacqueline exclaimed.

Jacqueline put her hand against the wall, feeling the cold, hard stone. Then, she reached to the other wall with her other hand and slowly moved forward as Zane followed.

She had her hands extended for some time before her hand disappeared into the wall. Immediately, she stopped and pulled back her hand out of instinct. She eyed the part of the wall her hand disappeared into, with Zane soon training on what she was seeing.

Eventually, Jacqueline put her hand back through the wall. As her hand disappeared, she could feel the cold air. She pulled her hand back once more and, hesitantly, put moved through the wall.

When she moved through the fake wall, the cold air completely took hold. Almost instantly, she began to shake from the temperature change, causing her to cross her arms and hold her arms tight to her body.

Zane followed and soon did the same. Then, Jacqueline could hear his teeth chattering behind her, due to his lack of adequate clothes.

"Flara."

In her hand, Jacqueline had summoned a small flame. As she held it, the feeling in her hands began to return. The flame was small enough to where, even without a scroll, she hardly used any Energy.

After the feeling returned, she held out the fire towards the niyan. At first hesitant, Zane took the small ball of fire into his hands. Just like with Jacqueline, the flame soon gave feeling back to his hands.

"Gods, it is so cold!" Zane exclaimed.

"Indeed," affirmed Jacqueline as she looked ahead.

The room they had entered was vast and full of ice. Mounted in the center of the room, there was a large statue that was surrounded by thick sheets of ice. The statue was tall—nearly hitting the ceiling—and looked to be of a human with two swords. Most of the details about the human were impossible to see through the ice, making it difficult for Jacqueline and Zane to determine who it was meant to be.

Around the statue, there were six tall pillars of ice. The ice surrounding the pillars was not as thick, allowing one to see the engravings on them. As the two ventured around the room, Jacqueline began to inspect the engravings to determine what they meant. The engravings were foreign and didn't seem to be of Atrian origin.

As Jacqueline inspected the pillars, Zane attempted to find an exit or any traps. There was little doubt that this room was trapped, but he began to wonder if they would be able to operate through the thick ice.

While the floor was made entirely from ice, a lot of it was covered in some sort of dirt, making it difficult to slip. However, even with the dirt and being cautious, Zane nearly slipped several times, possibly just due to his natural clumsiness.

Jacqueline was able to find information about the pillars in the book she borrowed, after some searching. It had mentioned that the symbols were from a form of Atrian that was lost to time, possibly deriving from the tongues of the Gods themselves. While it was impossible to know what the words said, the book was able to assist in translating what they meant to the normal tongue.

"Zane?" yelled out Jacqueline.

"Yeah, Jack?" Zane answered.

Silence.

"Jack?"

"Flara!"

Suddenly, a large, expansive flame appeared in the center of the room. As time passed, the flame grew larger and larger. The cold air had ceased, and the ice had begun to melt, leaving only large puddles of water underneath the two. The only ice still in the room was the random patches of ice in the corners of the expansive room and, quizzically, the large statue.

"What in the Hells, Jacqueline!?" cursed out the niyan. "You could've warned me; I almost got burned form that!"

"I told you before, Zane," Jacqueline fired back. "*Never* call me Jack."

"Whatever you say, Jack."

"Say that again, and you lose something you may need."

Zane gulped and stayed quiet. He trudged through the large puddles of water underneath him, stopping right next to the assassin as she looked at the large pillar in front of them. She would look at the statue for several moments, then back to the book, then back to the statue, studying.

The niyan began to look around the room; then something caught his eye. Towards the front of the room they entered from, he could see one of the pillars was discolored from the rest. The statues were of a colorless stone, but the one he saw was emanating a red color.

He approached the statue, looking it up and down for a few moments. The closer he got to the pillar, the hotter the air around him got. Around the pillar, water began to steam from its base into the air.

"Jacqueline?" asked Zane.

"Oh, you got it right this time," she acknowledged, still looking at her texts. "What is it?"

"Can you come here?"

Jacqueline looked over, and her eyes widened when she saw the discoloration. Quickly, she shifted through the ankle high water towards the red pillar. She studied it for some time, then flipped through the pages in her book. Eventually, she found the page whose symbols matched that of the pillar.

"Fire," she said underneath her breath.

"Fire?" quizzed Zane. "What do you mean?"

"Fire! Each of these pillars has a specific element with them. The one I was looking at was light, but, until now, I didn't realize what it meant. That would mean…"

She began to sift through the book once more, then eyed the pillar next to them. She compared the symbols in the book to the pillar for a few moments before she concluded what it was. Then, she held her hand out towards the pillar.

"Watara chifang!"

A small blue beam was summoned from her hands towards the pillar. After a few moments, the pillar began to turn blue. In doing so, the water surrounding it began to freeze slowly.

"The pillars react to the element used!" exclaimed Zane. "That's genius!"

Slowly, Jacqueline was able to decipher each of the other three pillars and cause them to react to the right elements. By the end of it, all six pillars were the correct color; fire was red, water was blue, wind was green, earth was brown, dark was black, and light was white. When the last pillar— dark—reacted to Jacqueline's spell, she heard a large crack behind them.

Jacqueline ran over to Zane, who was standing in front of the frozen statue, and watched as the ice began to crack further. As the cracking extended from the top to the base of the statue, the water within the room began to evaporate. The room felt muggy, humid, and, to Jacqueline, disgusting.

Sweat could already be felt going down their faces as they watched the ice continue to crack and fall to the stone floor below. Zane, still low on Energy, took several steps back as Jacqueline unsheathed her daggers. She got into her defensive stance as she stared at the large statue's icefall.

As the last chunk of ice fell, the statue's obsidian shown, with its ruby eyes reflecting the light in the room. On the back of the statue was a large black and red cloak that covered most, if not all, of their body. Additionally, they were hooded.

On their chest was the symbol the two had never seen before. The text that Jaqueline carried with her made no note of what the symbol was or what it meant. Just what was this statue meant to be for?

And, more importantly, how do they relate to the Lich?

CHAPTER VIII

The statue did not reveal any clues as to where they were to go next. The book Jacqueline had, as well, refused to provide the secrets they needed to continue their conquest into the tomb. Zane impatiently returned to the corridor they came from, unable to find another hidden door. For now, it seemed like they were stuck.

However, fatigue was starting to set in. Zane was often taking small breaks to recover enough Energy to continue his search, with Jacqueline slowly feeling her eyes grow heavy as she read. While it had been some time since the two saw the mighty sun Sacrilege, their bodies were telling them that it was time for rest.

Unfortunately, out of sheer ignorance or forgetfulness, they both forgot to bring their cloths and linen to sleep. Instead, they were forced to try and rest on the cold hard floor of the humid room.

The conditions they were in made it uncomfortable for the pair to sleep, but, eventually, they were able to drift into a deep slumber. With little fear of being attacked in their sleep—Jacqueline was a light sleeper—a protection spell was not cast on the two.

Zane was beginning to snore loudly, signalling that he was the first to fall asleep. Jacqueline could feel her mind begin to slow down and begin to wander into a deep sleep, only to feel it slightly interrupted by Zane's snoring.

———————

Jacqueline suddenly got up. The room was dark, but there was a small light illuminating from the six pillars, enough to give her the light needed to cast a light spell. When it was cast, she looked over to see that Zane wasn't there.

"Zane?" she asked, looking around for his companion.

It was then that she noticed that the light was doing very little to quell the darkness around her; it was still impossible to see several feet past her. She walked over to where Zane was, and began to look for any clues as to where he went. Unfortunately, there was nothing.

"Zane?" she cried out again.

She suddenly began to fear the worst.

Nothing but silence answered her. The humidity was no longer in effect, but there was still an unease in the room that she couldn't explain. Part of her felt like she was being watched, but another part of her felt like the assassin was in mortal danger.

"Hello?" she spoke to the surrounding darkness.

Still, nothing by silence. Was it anxiety? Was it fear? Or was it something else entirely? Those were the questions filling her mind, causing her to second guess everything.

As she moved around, she often hesitated thinking she had heard something, only to realize it was a rock or dirt she kicked. When the young assassin approached different parts of the large room, the light would follow her around, illuminating the path. However, there was still little in the room of note.

Jacqueline made her way over to the entrance of the room, quickly realizing it was sealed. Frantically, she felt around the wall, wondering if her memory was misplaced. After some time, she realized that she was stuck in this dark room—alone.

A hissing sound could be heard coming from the other side of the room. Upon hearing this, the assassin unsheathed her blades and took a defensive stance. She could feel her heart rate steadily grow higher as she waited to see what else was trapped with her.

Moments later, another hissing sound came from the same direction. If she wasn't mistaken, it sounded a lot like the rellagate she fought the previous day. However, unlike before, the lights were not disappearing with its presence.

"Flara quao!" commanded Jacqueline.

Suddenly, a large firebolt appeared in the air and was hurled towards the hissing sound. The bolt flew, only to be stopped by a wall. While the fire helped lighten the other part of the room, there was still nothing over there.

"Aka'ia zaia'to huam ata'ach… Why are you… Here?"

Jacqueline hardly moved a muscle as she scanned around the edges of the darkness, searching for the source of the voice. Several more hisses could be heard, but she was unable to determine where the voice originated.

"Okawa kria ohmi'ha, zalea… Why must you… Enter the domain of the darkest shadow?"

"Show yourself!" demanded Jacqueline.

Silence. All Jacqueline could do was tighten the grip on her blades, being patient as to wait for a reply from her guest. But, for some time, there was nothing.

"Zalea, akai zoma huam ata'ach… She will make this… Your tomb…"

Eventually, Jacqueline could see a small red light at the corner of her eye. She snapped her head up, only to see the light coming from the pupils of the gigantic statue placed in front of her.

"Show yourself, spirit!" she demanded once again.

"Meredith, Lichiam… Her power… Is beyond mortality…"

Jacqueline lowered her guard lightly, realizing that the statue posed little threat to her. Instead, she pointed the tip of her blade towards the head of the statue.

"Where is Zane?"

The statue would not answer for several moments, causing her to repeat herself in a desperate attempt for answers.

"Niya sao… He sleeps in the first… World…"

"The what?"

"Zaia'to… I am the architect… Of this forsaken place… I am Morokai, offspring of the Dark One…"

"Dark One? Sato?"

"Okia'oa… Erakai…"

The same Omni who betrayed his friends, resulting in the First Sin?

"Why am I here?" she eventually asked. "How do I find the Lich?"

"Meredith… Lichiam… She cannot be stopped… The seal cannot contain her any longer…"

"Then, what can I do? I can't exactly leave and let her grow stronger."

"The seal is weakening… Her return draws near…" answered the voice, after a few moments pause.

Jacqueline looked down at the ground, slowly processing what Erian was saying to her. She had thought, up to this point, that some being, some creature, was resurrecting Meredith from her death. But, now, that was far from the case. Her seal, the very thing preventing her return, is gone.

"How do I stop her?" she asked.

The edges of the room began to glow white, slowly enveloping the room in its embrace. Caught off guard, Jacqueline allowed the white light to overtake her body, praying it were all part of the vision she was encountering.

———

When the white light dissipated, Jacqueline was hovering over what seemed to be a battle between two mages. The two were battling over a large, burning plain as soldiers around them fought with swords and maces. The two continued to stare the other day, seeing who would move first.

On one side of the battlefield was a tall zichan, wielding two long swords of a craftsmanship Jacqueline had never seen before. They possessed a blue and gold robe, akin to the robes given to the spellcasters of today. On both of their ears, there was a large sapphire stone that shined brightly. Their eyes were slanted, with a large, bloody cut going down one of their sockets.

The other side of the battle had a familiar looking female, one with a single staff and a long red robe. Contrast to the defensive stance the zichan had; this woman had a certain elegance in her stance—as if she knew the zichan was no threat to her. Her eyes were a deep yellow color, with a smirk that begged to be stricken off her face. There was little doubt that this was Meredith, the Lich of Izaman. At least, before she earned that title.

But, where was this? This was obviously a vision, but what of? This was the first Jacqueline had ever experienced something such as this, but she had heard of such a thing occurring before—especially from her friend, Max.

"*Mortal,*" began the soon-to-be-Lich. "This is where your story ends!"

The zichan shook his head, not uttering another word. He kept his defensive stance, with both of his swords slowly glowing brighter with each passing moment.

"This is your last chance," she continued. "Surrender, and you will be spared. Otherwise, you will be forgotten like your ancestors."

"No," answered the zichan. "This is *your* last chance. Surrender, and you will be spared the torment of a hundred lifetimes, witch!"

"This world is doomed, *mortal*. The Gods you know speak blasphemy, the champions you follow are heretics, and your leaders are leading their cattle to their doom."

"I'm sorry… Meredith, but this is for the greater good. Goodbye, my love."

At once, both swords the zichan wielded began to glow white. The zichan then forced them both to the ground, forcing a giant shockwave to affect the area. As the shockwave expanded outward, soldiers from both sides of the battle fell to the ground. Grunting—and cries from falling on their weapons—could be heard throughout the battlefield.

At the epicenter, a giant tornado began, surrounding both the zichan and Meredith. The tornado began to glow different colors, changing through the different elements. As the tornado expanded into the heavens, the tornado began to constrict towards both combatants.

Before long, the tornado's color stopped and changed to a deep black—rivalling the black of the Darkening. Then, as quickly as the tornado appeared, it vanished. At the center of the battle, both the zichan and Meredith could not be seen— they had vanished.

Jacqueline began to search around, unable to find the exact location of them both. However, she could see the world begin to whiten around her once more. Then, all she could see was a white void.

When Jacqueline returned, she looked back up at the statue.

"I... Think I understand, now," she said.

"Meredith, Lichiam..." answered the voice. *"Her power is beyond that of mortals, and perhaps even the Gods... I*

sacrificed my soul… My heart… My spirit… To lock my love away forever. But not all magic lasts forever."

"I will finish what you started, then. Just tell me how."

"Zalea, zaia'to… To unlock the door, you must speak the name of the darkest shadow… Nay, the darkest of darkness incarnate. The root of the dark stems from that name."

Jacqueline looked to the side, trying to decide who the spirit was referring to. Was it, perhaps, Sato, the God of Death, Destruction, Disease, and Carnage? Or were they referring to Erakai, the betrayer of the Omni? She couldn't know for certain, but she had to mutter a name.

"Erakai."

The room began to shake violently upon hearing that name. Jacqueline fell to her knees, forcing her to push up against the base of the statue for some stability. Rocks from the ceiling began to collapse around her, boulders started to fall out of the walls, and she could hear cave-ins all around her.

The dust of the rocks falling was toxic, causing her to gag out of reflex. It was heavy and abundant, forcing her to use her tunic to filter out the dust. However, that proved worthless as the dust grew thicker and thicker.

Suddenly, she was choking. There was no oxygen entering her body, and it was responding in kind. She held her throat as tears began to flow down her cheeks. Her body attempted to cough, unable to remove the toxic dust from her system.

Then, her eyes began to grow heavy. They grew heavier and heavier as she could feel her mind begin to shut down. Up to now, she was attempting to figure out how to get out of this situation. This time, however, there was no solution—there was only death.

Jacqueline gasped for air as she woke from her sleep. She began to cough violently out of reaction, unable to open her eyes. Her mind was tricked into thinking the toxic dust was still in her, attempting to expel them from her system.

As she wheezed, she was able to open her eyes finally. Tears had clouded her ability to see, forcing her to rub her eyes quickly. When her vision was restored, she was relieved to see a worried Zane sitting across the room.

"A-are you alright?" he worryingly asked.

Jacqueline nodded a few times, coughing every few moments, in response. Zane shook his head and returned his gaze to a book that was placed in front of him.

"Must've been a Hells of a dream," he mentioned.

"It was... Vivid," she responded, coughing between words. "I think... It may have been a vision."

"A vision?"

Visions were said to be the manifestations of the Gods; an ability passed down to the mortals so that they, too, can see the events of yet to be. In the beginning, only certain beings—usually those who held extreme faith—were blessed with this power. These begins came to be known as the Seers.

And, as time went by, how one attained this ability became more difficult to understand. Today, it is rare to see an adult unlock this latent skill and be able to command it. It is often thought that many mortals held this power, but how to trigger it is impossible to determine.

Jacqueline had never had this dream, or possibly a vision, before—she never dreams. What she felt was vivid, foreboding, and dark. Everything that occurred in that dream she felt. Everything that happened she could see. She could remember every detail.

"Erakai," she muttered out loud.

The statue next to them began to shake, forcing Jacqueline and Zane to step back. Jacqueline unsheathed her swords, already encountering déjà vu from the vision she just received. Was the vision about to come true? Were they to suffocate in the darkness of the Lich's tomb, never to be found again?

As the statue shook, a light began to shine through it. It was a blinding light, forcing the pair to cover their eyes. The shaking only continued for a few moments more before it suddenly stopped.

Jacqueline was the first to uncover her eyes and was also the first to see what had happened to the statue. As her vision returned, she was able to see that the statue had disappeared entirely and, in its place, was a large sarcophagus.

"What in the Hells?" she cursed out loud.

"Is it safe to open them?" asked Zane.

"What? Yeah, yeah, you're safe. Look."

Zane opened his eyes, giving the same reaction as Jacqueline. They both approached the stone sarcophagus slowly, in case it was trapped. Once they realized that the stone in front of them wasn't, they began to dust the sides of it.

On both sides of the sarcophagus—to her surprise—was words written in the common language and not Atrian.

"'Even in darkness, I love thou,'" the assassin translated, slowly moving her hand across the text. "'Through... Eternity, through shadows, through the... Future, I shall forever. This is to the future of not just ourselves, but of our race.'"

"What?" asked Zane. "Who is this? What does this mean?"

Everything started to click in her mind; the vision, the sarcophagus, this tomb, the Lich of Izaman, all of it.

This was all a tragedy.

"This is the sarcophagus of Morokai," she answered, finally. "The loved one of the Lich, Meredith."

"Morokai? Loved one? Liches do *not* love, they are evil incarnate!"

"Meredith was once good," Jacqueline mentioned, snapping her head towards Zane. "Then, as with some good people, Sato got involved."

"Woah, woah, woah, wait a moment. Sato? *The* Sato?"

"Who else could I be referring to, Zane?"

"This is just… Crazy," Zane said as he went to sit down on a part of the broken statue. "This doesn't make sense to me."

"I had a vision," she mentioned to the niyan. "Morokai spoke to me, telling me how to beat the Lich—Meredith."

"Is it in that sarcophagus?" he asked, pointing towards the large stone in front of the pair where the statue once was.

Jacqueline dusted off the top of the sarcophagus lightly, able to see even more symbols. However, unlike the Atrian symbols, these were from another language she couldn't decipher. They were unlike the ones she saw in the book, as well, telling her that this is from a language long since lost.

Slowly, she put her hands by the lid of the sarcophagus. She budged slightly and noticed that the lid was extremely heavy. She pushed harder, but it was still unable to move. Jacqueline motioned for Zane to assist her, to which he did.

Together, the two began to push on the lid of the sarcophagus. It started to budge and, before long, the lid was pushed off from the top, falling to the floor.

They looked inside the sarcophagus, surprised to see not the mummified remains of Morokai, but two long, glowing swords. The hilt of the blades was curved slightly, to allow the wielder to use different styles. The handguard was plated gold, with small etchings engraved into it. As you looked up the blade, both made a note of the ancient, foreign symbols.

"What are they?" asked the niyan.

Jacqueline reached into the sarcophagus and grabbed both blades. She pulled them out and rose them up above her. She could feel the Energy in the room start to swirl towards her as they stayed in the air.

She could feel her soul start to gain more courage as time went on and she stared at the beautiful craftsmanship. There was a reason that Morokai showed her the vision and why he led her to unlock this sarcophagus.

"This, my friend," she said. "Is how we defeat the Lich."

CHAPTER IX

The hallway was long, dark, and creepy—at least, that is what Zane was thinking. Once Jacqueline picked up the twin blades from the sarcophagus, one of the walls began to collapse, showing a long passage to their destination.

This must be it, right? Jacqueline thought to herself.

Only the Gods knew how long the two had been inside of the Tomb of the Lich, and only they knew how much longer they had. It had felt like days, but it could easily have been hours; time was impossible to tell in the depths of this forsaken tomb.

"Do you think we're ready?" asked Zane, trying to spark a conversation between the two.

"I hope so, for all of our sakes," answered Jacqueline.

Ever since she got the twin blades, Jacqueline had been quieter; she was not as talkative. Zane just chalked it up to her extreme focus, but he felt like there was something else to it entirely. He might be paranoid, after all.

When they first began to traverse the long, dark hallway, Jacqueline, for a time, explained the vision she saw. She told of what Morokai had said to her, how she knew the swords were the key to defeating Meredith, and even the grim ending she experienced.

The only part of the vision they couldn't understand was the suffocation she had suffered. Visions, if experienced, often proved to be true. It begged the question if that part of the vision was incorrect... Or if that was their fate for protecting the realm from a terrible darkness.

Jacqueline stopped, as did Zane.

"What is-?"

"Shh."

Jacqueline had her finger up to her lips as she turned back to the niyan, then she snapped her head back forward. She heard something, but she didn't know if it was paranoia or if it was something else entirely. Was it another trap?

The two stayed silent, and still, for some time, then a crack was hard behind them. Jacqueline snapped backward to see a bright light flowing from the end of the hallway, and the floor disappearing.

"Run!" she screamed out as her eyes widened.

Without hesitation, Zane followed her, and the two ran as fast as they could down the hallway. With each step, another part of the floor behind them had fallen, consumed by a bright red light.

Jacqueline looked back several times, surprised to see that the niyan in his weakened state was keeping up. But, she could see that the collapsing floor was getting closer and closer to the pair. They weren't going fast enough!

"Faster, Zane!" she commanded.

Without another word, Jacqueline began to run as fast as she ever had, outracing Zane. It was becoming more and more obvious that Zane's lack of Energy was coming into play—he was slowing down.

"Zane!" she yelled behind her. "Don't give up! Keep running!"

"I'm trying, dammit!" he yelled back.

The collapsing floor was closing in. The hallway became more and more consumed by the red light, and the temperature was beginning to increase. It had to be a lava trap!

"Zane! Faster! I see the end of the hallway!"

Jacqueline pushed herself harder, bolting down the hallway. As an assassin, she was used to running at incredibly high speeds, but this was starting to wear on her body. To keep up her endurance, she was forced to use part of her Energy to supplement it.

When she got to the end of the hallway, she slid through the entrance, without looking ahead, and looked back to her friend.

Please, Gods, don't do this.

Zane was barely moving faster than the collapsing floor. Sweat was beaming down his head as it became more difficult to breathe. The niyan looked up to see his friend at the end of the hallway, which gave him the motivation he needed to push himself enough.

The floor was on his tail. He was now outpacing the collapse by a few stones, and he still had a hundred or so feet to go. He had no more Energy to spare, and he was at his limits. At any point, his legs—or his lungs—could give out.

"Zane, jump!"

Zane ran a few feet further and jumped as far as he could towards Jacqueline, just in time for the floor underneath him to give out. As he flew, it felt as if the world around them had started to slow down.

Jacqueline had to time this just right, otherwise Zane was a goner. She knew how to cast the

spell from her training with the Sixth Signet, but she did not have the scroll with her—it was still on Ramadier. She would need to use a lot of Energy, but she had to do this.

Zane began to descend, flailing his hands as he tried to reach for something. The rest of the floor had given out in front of him, leaving him nothing to grab to. Instead, under him, was a large pool of molten rock, ready to burn him to ash.

"Floa!"

Suddenly, Zane stopped his descent and was flown back into the air, just shy of hitting the ceiling of the hallway.

With the forward momentum he had, the spell was just enough for him to fly through the end of the hallway, falling onto Jacqueline. Both slid several feet before stopping, with Jacqueline underneath the niyan.

"Ow," remarked the niyan.

"Zane, can you get off, please?" she asked politely.

Zane opened his eyes, only to realize his head was positioned right next to her head, practically almost kissing her as he got up. Quickly, he jumped back.

"I'm sorry!" he apologized, holding his hands together. "Don't kill me!"

Jacqueline stumbled as she got up, an aftereffect of own weakened state. Once she held herself up, she held out a hand to the still apologizing niyan.

"It's fine," she assured. "I'm not that much of a bitch."

Zane gave a small smile and reached up to grab her hand. As he brushed himself off from the two near-death experiences he suffered, Jacqueline began to look around.

"Where are we?" he asked, still looking at his tunic.

Silence.

"Jacqueline?" he asked again.

Silence, once more.

"Jacqueline are you... Woah..."

Ahead of the two, at the center of the room, was a large sarcophagus, much like the one Morokai had. At the different ends of the room, there were six differently colored chains latched onto the sarcophagus. All, but the red chain, was severed.

Laughing could be heard through the room. Jacqueline unsheathed her new twin swords, assuming a defensive stance, as Zane looked around, confused.

"Welcome, heroes," began to voice. *"This is my dominion, my home, my tomb."*

"Show yourself, Meredith!" commanded Jacqueline.

The voice only chuckled.

"As you wish."

A large beam of light appeared at different sides of the room, soon converging over the sarcophagus. The air in the room had drastically changed from calmness to that of severe power. Electricity could be felt roaming through the air as the light grew more intense. After a few moments, the light shifted towards the red chain, instantly severing it.

The light disappeared, but the intense power remained. The lid on the sarcophagus began to move, and a violent red light was erupting from within it, along with another dark laugh.

"At last! After one-thousand years, I have returned!" began the voice, echoing across the chamber. *"Ethos shall, once more, suffer for what the Gods have done! Ethos shall, once more, fall into eternal shadows for their sins! Ethos*

106

shall, once more, become the dominion—the rightful throne—to the Lich of Izaman, Meredith Graha!"

Zane took several steps back, almost falling over the ledge into the lava pool. There was no turning back, now. This was it—become heroes and live or die and let darkness rule once more.

The red light's intensity stopped. A skeletal hand appeared from within the tomb on both sides of the sarcophagus. Slowly, a skeletal figure rose from within the tomb, drenched in tattered red robes and a large wooden staff.

The skeleton only chuckled.

"What?" they asked. *"Blinded by my beauty? My magnificence? My majesty?"*

Jacqueline took a step forward, with both twin swords pointed to the Lich. The Lich, in response, tilted their skeletal skull, and another dark laugh erupted from them.

"Wh-what's so funny?" asked Zane, scared.

"You possess the twin blades but know not how to use them."

"I'm a quick learner," Jacqueline snapped back.

Again, the Lich laughed and began to float into the air. As they floated into the air, a shield could be seen going around her. The shield began as red, but it soon changed colors to that of the other elements. Then, the colors began to blend until it was only white.

"Show me, then, and suffer."

The room started to change to a dark red color, with bolts of lightning being sent across the room. Jacqueline and Zane jumped to opposite sides of the room and began to dodge the electricity. Jacqueline began to jump off the walls, diving out of the way from the Lich's attacks, while Zane ran across the room as best as his body would allow.

Zane was still winded from his run across the hallway, putting him at a disadvantage. Luckily for him, it seemed as if Meredith was focusing more on Jacqueline—most likely due to her having the swords. Still, he was being pushed far beyond what he could endure—he had to hide.

Meanwhile, Jacqueline jumped off the wall and plunged her swords towards the Lich. Meredith only smiled as the assassin approached her. When Jacqueline was mere feet away, a shockwave sent her flying back, causing her to cry out in pain.

"I don't think you know who you're dealing with, girl," taunted the Lich.

Jacqueline slowly got up, just in time to evade another blast of electricity from her foe. After dodging, and limping, for a few moments, the room began to violently change colors. The burst of colors began to make the assassin feel sick, causing her to close her eyes to avoid the change—she had to rely on her other senses more, now.

When she closed her eyes, Jacqueline heard the roar of a bear go across the room. She opened her eyes wide, looking towards a giant bear jumping towards the Lich. The Lich, caught off guard, was knocked to the floor.

"Zane!" Jacqueline cried out.

The colors of the room stopped, returning to the normal room they were in previously. Zane, in his bear form, looked down at the Lich as they began to slowly rise from the ground. He roared once more and moved towards attacking Meredith once more.

This time, the Lich was prepared. She forced her palm forward, sending Zane back towards the front of the room. He roared in pain and slid several feet, barely stopping himself from falling over the edge into the lava pit below.

"Zane, no!"

Jacqueline ran over to assist her friend when Meredith teleported in front of her. The Lich's bones were cracked from the impact of the bear's attack. Their previously Abyss-black eye sockets erupted into a deep crimson, looking down at the assassin.

Jacqueline began to rise into the air. She felt the feeling in her body cease, unable to move any of her limbs. Her heart rate began to rise, realizing she was helpless against the Lich of Izaman, whose face slowly went towards Jacqueline.

"You mortals are all the same," the Lich said. *"You know not of the past. You are ignorant of the future. You are pathetic."*

Jacqueline couldn't respond, as she began to flinch. The pressure was starting to be applied to her body, especially her chest. With each moment that passed, it grew harder and harder to breathe.

"You worshipped deities who care not for you," they continued. *"And, unfortunately for you, they are no longer here."*

Jacqueline could no longer breathe. Was this the suffocation her vision entailed?

Then, all she heard was another roar of a bear. At the same time, Jacqueline fell to the ground and began to wheeze and cough. When she looked up, she could see a bloodied bear fighting off against the Lich.

Before Meredith had an opportunity to counter-attack, Zane took several more swipes at the Lich, knocking her backwards. Jacqueline, several times, could see a spell begin to charge up, only to lose concentration from the bear's relentless attacks.

Jacqueline rose up—limping heavily—while grabbing her twin blades. When she stood up completely, she looked down to see that both blades were glowing. The glowing was like the glowing she saw in the vision with Morokai.

Is this it?

There was only one way to know for sure.

The assassin put together the rest of her Energy and charged towards the Lich. Zane looked over towards Jacqueline, giving a moment's pause from his attack on the Lich. A moment later, and the bear began to cry out in pain once again.

Jacqueline looked, her eyes widening, as she saw a large blade of fire strike through Zane's upper torso. She never had a chance to scream out. Instead, she leapt forward towards the Lich that struck at him.

At that moment, the swords' light brightened the room entirely. The light was blinding, forcing Jacqueline to close her eyes as she felt her body sore through the air. Then, a moment later, she could hear the swords scraping against bone.

She opened her eyes, only to still be blinded by the lights. Eventually, through her eyelids, she could see the light begin to slowly dim around her, allowing the assassin to open them once more.

When she opened them, both blades were pierced through the upper chest of the Lich. Her eyes crimson red eyes were dark, lifeless.

Jacqueline pulled away, taking the swords out of the Lich as the skeleton fell to the floor. To make sure it wasn't a trick, she kicked the skeleton as hard as she could, sending the bones across the room. Then, she noticed that the air in the room had calmed—the Lich's magic was seemingly gone.

"Zane!" she cried out, turning around to her wounded friend.

Zane had already transformed back into his niyan form, but a large vertical could be seen in his right chest. Jacqueline slid as she got close, quickly reaching into her bag and putting the healing scroll on her wounded friend.

"Heal!"

The niyan began to heal, and their chest wound began to slowly close. However, there was a problem: Jacqueline was completely out of Energy, she had almost nothing else to spare.

"Zane! Come on, stay with me. I'll get you out of here, I swear on my life."

Zane wasn't responding to her calls and shakes. His breathing had grown thin, and his pulse was irregular. His eyes were closed, and his body was lifeless.

For the first time in a long time, Jacqueline could feel a tear fall down her face. It fell and hit the niyan on the cheek, then a stream of tears started to fall. Her body began to shake as she grabbed her friend, holding him close to her.

"I'm sorry," she whispered into his ear, sobbing. "I'm sorry for everything."

That's when it hit her: she had one more thing she could do. It was dangerous, and it was forbidden, but it was the only way. If she concentrated hard enough, she could transfer her life essence to her Energy. She would lose part of her remaining lifespan, but then he would be saved!

"I have to do this," she whispered to herself.

She got up and sat next to the niyan. The adventurer took several deep breaths. Before long, she took complete control of her emotions, focusing on the Energy she had left. She could feel it slowly begin to increase the harder she concentrated. Then, she lost it when she heard a familiar voice.

"Ja-Jack…"

Jacqueline looked down, seeing one of Zane's eyes looking up at her, though barely. She crouched down and held him close to her, already feeling her tears beginning to return.

"Give me a little longer, Zane," she said. "Just a little longer, and I'll save you!"

Zane faintly shook his head. His lips moved, but no words escaped from his mouth. While she couldn't hear it, she knew what he was trying to say: "No."

"I have to save you!" Jacqueline cried out. "This was *our* adventure, Zane! I'm not leaving you to die!"

Zane faintly shook his head again, then pointed behind the assassin. When Jacqueline looked behind, her face, full of sorrow and regret, changed to that of hatred and vengeance. She could feel something begin to overtake her soul, something pushing her far more than she thought possible. She could feel a powerful Energy consume her.

In front of the assassin was the Lich, reassembling her bones. A small, cyclone of magic could be seen surrounding the Lich and her apparent resurrection. Moments later, her skeletal form had been completely restored.

Jacqueline looked down at her swords, and saw they were glowing. She sprinted towards the Lich and began to attack her as fast as possible. Each jab, strike, slash, and plunge was blocked by a magical forcefield.

Jacqueline, however, pushed herself further. She began to attack in multiple directions at once, forcing the Lich to focus on two separate angles. Her attacks began to get faster and faster, eventually forcing the Lich to fall back several feet.

She looked at the swords again and saw that the twin blades were glowing bright. Seeing this, she took another plunge at the Lich before jumping back.

"You cannot stop the darkness," assured Meredith. *"For I am infinite, for I am eternity!"*

"I don't need to stop you," told Jacqueline. "I just need to make sure you never return."

The Lich chuckled in response.

Jacqueline could see glyphs appear around the room, each of which possessing a different element. She had seen this sort of spell before, but she had never been on the receiving end of it. If her next move didn't work, this was the end.

She put her swords together and closed her eyes. In one swift movement, she then plunged the swords towards the stone underneath her. Suddenly, a large tornado started to form around them.

"No!" screamed the Lich. *"This is impossible! Who told you of this!?"*

"I did."

Jacqueline looked behind her to see the same spirit who assisted her before, the very same who used the blades to defeat Meredith over a thousand years ago—Morokai. His spirit was a dark red color, akin to the ethereal form of the Lich she saw earlier.

"You!" screamed the Lich. *"Why are you here!?"*

"To finish what I started, my love," answered Morokai, standing right next to Jacqueline.

The tornado surrounding Jacqueline, Meredith, Morokai, and the wounded Zane began to change colors rapidly. Each of the elemental colors could be seen for a moment before it flashed to another color. Slowly, the tornado approached the four.

"Jacqueline," said the spirit of Morokai.

"Yeah?" Jacqueline answered, glancing to her left.

"Thank you, for everything."

Morokai's spirit moved forward towards the Lich, who began to move backwards. The tornado started to surround them both, with Jacqueline and Zane escaping the rapid winds from inside the cyclone.

The room was beginning to shake rapidly as stone, rubble, and dirt began to cave in around the two. Jacqueline looked around, then quickly ran over to protect her wounded friend from attacks. By the time she reached him, the room had almost completely caved-in.

Jacqueline, fearing this was the end, closed her eyes, holding her friend close. The rumbling of the room continued for some time, then it stopped. She didn't want to open her eyes, in fear that she had passed away from the collapse.

Had they died as heroes?

Jacqueline finally found the courage to open her eyes. At first, she was blinded by a sort of bright light, causing her to reclose them. Then, the sounds of birds chirping, wind rustling across the grass, and the other sounds of nature overwhelmed her.

Once she opened her eyes, she instantly knew where she was at: just outside of Wao.

"Hold on, Zane," she said to her friend, doing her best to pick him up. "We're home."

EPILOGUE

Zane was lucky; if he hadn't shown up when he did, his wounds would've been irreversible. The small amount of Energy Jacqueline used to heal him was enough to cauterize the wound and prevent him from bleeding out.

Still, the niyan was in a coma for almost two weeks as he healed. Regularly—at least three times a day—Jacqueline would stop by and see how her friend was doing, with the healers giving no update to his condition.

It was difficult, at first, for Jacqueline to get the healers to assist her friend. Since Wao was in Zalzabar, they feared repercussions from the Order. However, with Wao being an irregular target of Order patrols, Jacqueline was able to get them to agree in assisting her in exchange for Rubees.

During the last two weeks, she worried more than she ever had before. Her wounds from the battle with the Lich of Izaman were minor compared to what Zane suffered, but he saved her twice during the descent into the tomb.

All she could do was worry.

At the end of the two-week period was the first time she saw him awake. As soon as Jacqueline saw he was awake, she rushed over and hugged him gingerly as to avoid hurting him.

"Zane, you're awake!" she said happily.

"He-hey Jacqueline," he said, hugging her back. "Wh-what happened?"

"We did it, Zane! The Lich is gone!"

"Ho-how did we get out of there?"

Jacqueline hesitated for a moment. It was possible that Morokai teleported them both out of the tomb, but she didn't know for sure. What happened, exactly, was a blur to her, as well.

"I-I don't know," she said, shaking her head. "Morokai?"

Zane nodded his head, resting it back on the comfortable white pillow he was provided. The two stayed silent for some time, enough that one of the healers inside of the building had come by to check on their patient. After checking his pulse and asking a few questions on his pain factor, they left the room again.

"So, what now?" asked Zane, after some time had passed.

Again, Jacqueline hardly knew how to answer. Until he was fully healed, she couldn't leave. At any moment, the Order could stop by Wao. If they found the niyan, there was no telling what they could do to him.

"Just wait, I guess," she answered.

"Waiting is not something you usually do, Jacqueline."

"What else am I to do, Zane?"

Zane just shrugged, then gave a small smile. Jacqueline couldn't help but smile back; it was the first time she had in some time. The two looked outside to the beautiful forests just outside of the window, mesmerized by nature's beauty.

"I did get something," he said.

Jacqueline turned away and looked at Zane, who was already reaching down to one of his pockets. He rummaged through one of them for a moment, then reached for his other pocket, finding what he was looking for. He pulled it out and presented it in front of Jacqueline.

The stone was a small brown stone, looking to be made quartz. The stone was mostly round, with very few jagged edges. On both sides of the rock, there was the symbol of the element of earth.

Jacqueline took the stone in her hand but was unable to figure out what it was. She had never seen such a stone before and was wondering it held some magical properties due to the inscriptions on the side.

"Wh-where'd you get this?" she asked, still inspecting the stone.

"Found it during our fight with the Lich," he mentioned. "I retreated at the beginning and found it lying down next to the sarcophagus."

"It just looks like some sort of random stone."

"Maybe. At least, it is a momento of our victory, eh?"

Jacqueline gave back the stone and smiled.

A victory, it was.

————

Some months had passed since the battle against the Lich. Once Zane was strong enough, the two went their separate ways. Jacqueline returned to her adventuring throughout Ayasha, and Zane returned to Hian to be with his friends—it had been a long time since he last saw them.

On the journey back to Hian, the niyan encountered a major thunderstorm that forced him to retreat several miles to the nearest town—the open plains of Leo were not a suitable place for anyone to hide from a major storm. Once he ran back, he was able to find an inn on the side of the road. Luckily for him, the innkeepers couldn't care less that he was a niyan—if he had the Rubees.

At one of the corners, the niyan was eating dried-out meat and several glasses of ale when someone approached his table. At first, he didn't look up, thinking maybe they were part of the Order. But, after several moments, he realized he had to say something.

"May I help you?" he asked, without looking up.

"Yes, I am looking for someone," said a female.

"Who?"

"A man called Zane. Have you heard of him?"

Zane hesitated. Was he already found out? Did the innkeeper sell him out? This was bad. *Really* bad.

"A-and if I have?" he asked, stuttering.

The woman sat down in front of him. The beautiful woman had raven-colored hair, with a black dress to match. Her ears were pointed, an easy indication she was a zichan. On both of her shoulders, there were large golden rings. Her blue eyes, however, pierced right into his soul. Zane hardly knew how to talk due to her beauty.

"I'm looking for something he may have," she answered with a smirk.

What do I have that she wants?

Zane tried to look directly at the zichan but was forced to look to the side out of embarrassment. Whenever he dared to look up at her again, he could still see her smirk and piercing eyes. He knew she knew who he was.

"What do you want?" he asked. "I don't want any trouble."

"Trouble?" she asked, chuckling. "No, on the contrary, I am a collector of sorts. I've been searching for rare artifacts of ages past."

"And you think I have something?"

"Correct," said the zichan, nodding her head.

There was only one thing that Zane possessed that could attract her attention: the brown stone he got from the Lich of

Izaman months prior. Was it really an artifact? He never realized it was that important; but, then again, he wasn't the most gifted in spellcraft either.

He reached into his pocket and pulled out the brown stone, then placed it on the table. The zichan's eyes lit up, and her smirk grew into a smile as she inspected the stone. Zane could've sworn he saw the stone, for a moment, light up. Could that mean this woman was a spellcaster?

"Yes," she said out-loud after moments of inspecting. "This is *exactly* what I've been searching for! How much do you want for it?"

Zane just thought it was an ordinary stone until just now; how was he supposed to put a price on it? Either way, this meant that he could barter more Rubees off of the zichan, knowing it is that important to her.

"Two-hundred thousand," he demanded.

"Deal!" she said, reaching into her bag without hesitation.

Zane's eyes lit up; he wasn't expecting a deal, he figured he would have to barter with the zichan for some time. The woman went through her bags, eventually finding a large coin pouch. She placed it on the table, untied the knot, and poured it onto the table.

She counted the golden pieces out-loud from one to two-hundred. Rubees had three variations: a copper Rubee was worth one, a silver Rubee was worth a hundred, and a golden Rubee was worth a thousand. After several moments, she pushed two-hundred golden pieces towards the niyan who, for the entire time, had his mouth wide open.

"I-is that stone that important to you!?" he asked, still in shock at the revelation.

She only smirked at him for a few moments before getting up and grabbing her bags. She held the brown stone in her hand for a moment, then reached down and grabbed three more stones—a red, blue, and green one.

"Very," she said, smiling. "This is the key to everything."

Every light has a dark side...
Every flower has its thorns...

———————————

ACKNOWLEDGEMENTS

And that wraps up the second story in the *Illiad* universe! I really hope you guys enjoy this story, as it talks about a character I was extremely fond of in the first book. There are many more stories to tell, as with all the heroes of the Expedition, and I may visit more of them one day (maybe an anthology?)!

Before we wrap this up, I would like to thank my mother and friends who have been supporting me this entire way. When I was much younger, I aspired to write stories in all sorts of mediums (such as self-made comic books or through machinima), and they have been with me every step of the way! Thank you guys so much, and love you guys!

Onto the next!
-Clinton

ABOUT CLINTON REEL

Clinton Reel is a devoted indie author formerly of speedrunning "fame," with multiple records through several franchise—most notably the *Tony Hawk's Pro Skater* series. *The Illiad Chronicles* is a culmination of years of work to create a dark fantasy world that is both familiar and unpredictable. When he isn't writing, he is an IT technician who is seeing a degree in Cybersecurity. Along with writing, his hobbies include learning about technology, creating YouTube videos with friends, and even reading.

He was last seen searching for something somewhere in the middle of nowhere.

BOOKS BY CLINTON REEL

The Illiad Chronicles: Book I – Origins

The Illiad Chronicles – The Lich of Izaman

The Illiad Chronicles – The Last Rite
(Coming October 2018 – Free for mailing list subscribers)

The Illiad Chronicles: Book II – The Eternal Night
(Coming December 2018)

CONNECT WITH CLINTON REEL

Website: https://clintonreel.com

Facebook: https://facebook.com/thereelclinton

Twitter: https://twitter.com/clintonreel

Mailing List: https://clintonreel.com/mailinglist

Printed in Great Britain
by Amazon

12409030R00082